Last Walk Home

by the same author:

EVERY SECOND THURSDAY
ADD A PINCH OF CYANIDE

EMMA PAGE

Last Walk Home

WALKER AND COMPANY
NEW YORK

First published in the United States of America in 1983
by the Walker Publishing Company, Inc.
ISBN: 0-8027-5491-0
Library of Congress Catalog Card Number: 82-51308
Printed in the United States of America
10 9 8 7 6 5 4 3 2 1

For
Rosemary and Anthony
with love
(Not forgetting Daniel, Lucy and Oliver)

CHAPTER 1

In the front bedroom of Ivydene, on the outskirts of Cannonbridge, Lisa Schofield lay fast asleep with her long blonde hair spread out over the pillows. In the muted light her peachdown skin had a faintly golden quality and her bare shoulders gleamed against the lacy top of her trousseau nightdress.

She dreamed she was learning to ride a bicycle, laughing and squealing, falling off every few yards. Someone held the saddle as she climbed on again, a man's hand, firm and strong.

'Don't let me fall, Derek!' she cried out to her husband in the dream, although she knew without turning that it wasn't Derek but her father who held her safe.

Beside her in the big double bed Derek gathered himself up into a ball, tucking his head down towards his belly, trying to ward off his dream pursuers. They were gaining on him, crowding in on him, brandishing broken boughs—

Lisa turned over suddenly, flinging an arm across his face. He woke with a start of terror and leapt up with his heart pounding. 'A-ah!' he cried aloud.

He came wide awake and saw the shadowy outlines of the furniture, the mahogany tallboy, the bow-fronted chest of drawers. He drew a long shuddering breath—it was all right, he was safe in bed at Ivydene. He'd moved into the house on his marriage a few months ago; it had been Lisa's home for seven years before that, she had lived there with her older sister Janet and their mother.

Ivydene didn't yet feel like home to Derek but at least the sprigged wallpaper and chenille curtains of the bedroom greeted him as familiar acquaintances, if not old friends. His heart began to slacken its rapid beat.

The yellow sunlight of late July stole in through a gap in the curtains. He glanced at the bedside clock. Five minutes to six. If he lay down again he'd probably oversleep—and he daren't risk being late for work, particularly not on a Monday morning. Things were already dicey enough at the Cannonbridge Mail Order Company without his making the boss an outright present of an excuse for cutting down on staff.

He eased his way out from under the bedclothes, found his dressing-gown and slippers and went from the room with accustomed noiselessness; he was always up long before Lisa.

At the head of the stairs sunlight streamed in through an uncurtained stained-glass window, throwing shifting patterns of colour on to the landing, luminous pools of amber and green, rose and blue, as a wandering breeze rippled the tall trees in the garden.

He went softly down to the kitchen, comfortable and old-fashioned, he crossed to the window and drew back the flowered curtains.

'A nice cup of tea,' he said aloud; the words had a cosy, reassuring sound. He filled the kettle and put it on to boil. As he turned from the stove he met his own gaze in the mirror that hung to one side of the fireplace.

An unremarkable face, not bad-looking in a nineteen-thirties bandleader way. His brown eyes stared back at him, large, habitually anxious.

He was thirty-seven years old but had the air of being older. His light brown hair had a strong natural crimp that he'd fought for years to subdue, only to discover now on the verge of middle age that it had suddenly become fashionable. The growth was beginning to recede from his temples and nowadays his exploring fingers could locate a treacherous spot of thinning on the crown.

While he waited for the kettle to boil he unlocked the

back door and went out into the garden. Ivydene was a solidly-built Edwardian villa standing on the edge of Hadleigh, a semi-rural suburb of Cannonbridge; until fifty years ago Hadleigh had been an independent village.

The garden was large enough to stroll about in and gave a pleasant sense of space and seclusion. He plucked a weed here and there, lifted a wayward strand of a rambler rose and draped it over a neighbouring stem — he must remember to get a ball of garden twine in the lunch-hour. A fine climbing rose, trained along a trellis and over an arch, was just coming into flower, the blooms a deep soft peach tipped with cream. He selected a bud with care, the petals just about to unfurl, free from the smallest blemish. He carried it back to the kitchen and put it in a glass of water.

He made the tea, poured himself a cup and stood at the window drinking it, looking out at the tranquil garden, thinking about Lisa and his marriage, his new life at Ivydene.

There were moments when he felt as if it was all a dream; this struck him most often at work. He sat at the same desk, followed the same routine, nothing there was changed. But it seemed to him sometimes in odd disturbing flashes that he must shortly wake to find that home was still a cramped bedsitter in a down-at-heel quarter of Cannonbridge and Lisa no more than a beguiling face glimpsed in a bus queue.

She had married him two days after her eighteenth birthday, very much against the wishes of her sister. Janet was eleven years older than Lisa and was now her only close relative; their mother, Mrs Marshall, had died some months before the marriage, leaving Janet as legal guardian to Lisa till she came of age.

'You're surely not going to rush into marriage with the first man who's paid you any serious attention,' Janet had warned Lisa. 'It's madness at your age.' Particularly when the intended bridegroom was nearly twenty years older than Lisa and was possessed of assets and prospects so meagre as to be practically invisible.

Derek poured himself another cup and returned to the window. He had been overwhelmed by the dead set Lisa had made at him when they first met. She was then only a little over sixteen and had just left school. Mrs Marshall had wanted her to stay on to take a secretarial course but Lisa would have none of it — and when it came to a battle between Lisa and her mother Lisa usually won. She had been born eight months after her father's death and Mrs Marshall had always cosseted and cherished her second daughter, regarding her as a poor fatherless child to whom the world owed a great deal.

So Lisa threw her school hat in the dustbin, gave her blazer to a jumble sale and then went out and took the first job she could find. This turned out to be at the Cannonbridge Mail Order Company where Derek Schofield daily bent his head over columns of figures. In a matter of days the supper-time conversation at Ivydene became peppered with Derek's name and within another two or three weeks Lisa was declaring herself madly in love with him.

Both Mrs Marshall and Janet fervently hoped the attachment would wither and die as Lisa grew up and got some sense, but in spite of their opposition — or more probably because of it — she became unshakably determined to marry him. Her mother's death did nothing to weaken this determination and six months after her mother's funeral, on a fine spring morning, marry him she did — in the Cannonbridge register office with no friends or relatives present, and two cleaners called in to act as witnesses. Derek was swept up out of his poky bedsitter into the spacious comfort of Ivydene.

Janet Marshall was a schoolteacher, at that time teaching in the neighbouring village of Stanbourne, catching the bus every morning from a stop fifty yards up the road from Ivydene.

When Lisa and Derek returned from their Easter honeymoon in Tangier, Lisa was astounded to discover that Janet had moved out of Ivydene two days earlier. Not only that, but she'd given up her teaching post at Stanbourne and found herself another at Longmead, a village a few miles away. She was renting a small farm cottage close to the Longmead school, had removed a quantity of furniture, china and linen from Ivydene and was already comfortably installed in her new home.

Lisa didn't stop to unpack her bags but at once commanded Derek to drive her over to Rose Cottage.

'You never said a word about all this!' she stormed at her sister. 'You planned it all behind my back!'

'You chose to get married against my wishes,' Janet said calmly. 'I saw no reason to consult you about my own intentions.' Derek had stood by, mute and forgotten.

He stared out now at the dewy garden, brilliant in the glittering sunlight. Until Lisa came along he'd managed well enough on what he earned, he had even been able to save. There had been difficulties of course, but nothing he couldn't handle.

And then Lisa took control of his existence. 'You're being exploited,' she told him. 'You don't value yourself properly. You should be getting much more than they're paying you.' Easy enough to rectify. All he had to do was approach the boss with righteous confidence and point these matters out to him.

And, fired by Lisa's total certainty, Derek, shortly after returning from his honeymoon, still a little drunk from the North African sunshine and the astonishing pleasures of marriage, did actually walk in through the manager's door and put these points to him.

Unfortunately the manager didn't share Lisa's opinion. He informed Derek in loud clear tones that it was only by a miracle the firm was surviving at all, he was currently giving serious thought to the question of redundancies. 'If you're not satisfied,' he added, 'you've been here long enough to know where the door is.'

And that was that. Unemployment was high in Cannonbridge and still rising; there was certainly no massive demand for clerks approaching middle age.

Derek daren't tell Lisa he'd failed but allowed her to believe his efforts had been successful. 'My salary's being raised from the beginning of next month,' he told her, in the mad hope that something would happen to rescue him before his savings finally ran out. The greater part of these had already been swallowed up by his courtship and honeymoon, above all, by that wildly extravagant North African honeymoon; he had had no idea until then that it was possible for two people to spend so much money in fourteen days. And week by week the relentless expenses of his new life bit savagely into what was left of his nest-egg. He felt himself beset these days by problems, every one of them relating at some point to money. And in his dreams now the feet were getting closer.

Lisa had given up her job before the wedding and appeared to have no intention of ever again darkening the door of any place of employment. She was in any case now three months pregnant and as a consequence exempt in her own eyes from all but the very lightest endeavours.

He turned from the window, suddenly hungry, and made himself some toast. He sat down at the table, buttered the toast and smeared it with marmalade. He took a thoughtful bite.

Until his marriage he'd had scarcely any idea how expensive it was to run a house. Before he took to bedsits he had lived with his father in an old rented terrace house in a seedy area of Westfleet, a small town twenty-five miles from Cannonbridge; he had been born and brought up in the house.

Derek was an only child. His mother had run off with a neighbour when he was six years old and there had never been any other woman in the life of the deserted father and son.

His father—now dead—had been a labourer in the yard of a builder's merchant in Westfleet. He was out of doors in all seasons and as time went by he became afflicted with chronic bronchitis. 'Don't do what I've done,' he warned Derek when the time came for him to leave school. 'Get yourself a job that'll shelter you from the weather, one that'll keep your hands clean.' And that much at least Derek had managed to do. Lowly as his status was at Cannonbridge Mail Order, it had always seemed an achievement to him—until his marriage.

The bronchitis finally carried his father off when Derek was nineteen. 'I haven't amounted to much,' he said to Derek on the day before he died. 'You've got your whole life before you. Watch out you don't end up like me.' His gaze wandered round the dismal bedroom. 'I've left you everything.' Everything amounted to forty-odd pounds in the post office, some tools, a cupboardful of cheap clothes and a few sticks of worthless furniture.

The landlady didn't wait for the earth to settle over his grave before she marched round to the terrace house.

'I want you out of here inside a fortnight,' she informed Derek. 'I'm going to do this place up and sell it.'

She knew her man; Derek moved out at once without protest, almost with apology, into the first of his bedsits.

Now he blinked away the memories with a jerk of his head. He finished his toast and went over to the dresser, pulled open a drawer and took out a handful of bills. He sat down at the table to study the figures although the amounts were accurately burned into his brain. He clenched a fist and dug it into his chin, frowning down at the papers, trying to think of some way out of his difficulties. At last he blew out a long breath and stood up. 'Something's got to be done,' he said aloud.

In the meantime, in the big double bed upstairs, Lisa would be beginning to stir. He made a fresh pot of tea, found a clean linen cloth and smoothed it on to a tray. He poured a cup of tea and set it on the tray beside a small plate of biscuits and the peach-coloured rosebud in its glass of water. He carried the tray carefully upstairs to Lisa.

She woke and stretched like a cat and her long blonde hair fell back against the pillows. She smiled at him and held out her cheek for a kiss.

She drank some tea and nibbled at a biscuit, then she reached for the packet of cigarettes on the bedside table.

'I really think you ought to try to give them up,' Derek said apologetically. 'You know what the doctor said.'

She pulled a face. 'The doctor's an old woman.' She took out a cigarette and he lit it for her; she inhaled deeply. 'The doctor we had in Ellenborough smoked all the time.' The Marshalls had lived in Ellenborough, a large town forty-five miles away, before they moved to the Hadleigh suburb of Cannonbridge.

Outside there was the sound of feet on gravel, the click of the letterbox. 'That might be a letter from Janet,' Lisa said. 'Do go down and see.' There was only one post a day now in Hadleigh. Lisa had written to Janet again last week, asking her to come over as soon as the school term ended on Friday, stay as long as she liked.

Derek went downstairs to the hall. Three envelopes lay in the wire cage at the back of the door. The first was postmarked Cannonbridge, addressed to Lisa in the bold handwriting of her friend Carole Gardiner. The second was an advertising circular, and the third—he drew a long breath and ripped it open, running his eye rapidly over the sheet, biting deep into his lip as he read, unaware of any sensation of pain. He stood frowning down at the letter and then went swiftly into the sitting-room and knelt by the grate.

He pushed aside the tapestry firescreen that had been worked by Mrs Marshall, struck a match and set fire to the letter and its envelope. When they were both thoroughly consumed he ground the ashes into dust with the poker and replaced the screen. He got to his feet and went back upstairs.

'Nothing from Janet,' he said as he entered the bedroom. On his tongue he could taste the blood from his bitten lip. 'But Carole Gardiner's written to you.'

'When are we going to have the phone put in?' Lisa said impatiently as she took the letter he held out. 'It's such a nuisance, all this letter-writing.'

'There's a waiting-list for phones,' he said. He had no idea if this was so; he had made no application for a phone. What he did know with bleak certainty was that he could afford neither the installation fee nor the quarterly expenses.

'You couldn't ring Janet even if we did have a phone,' he reminded Lisa. There was no phone at Rose Cottage and Janet didn't intend to have one put in.

Lisa's full red mouth looked sulky. 'What's your letter?' she asked after a moment's silence.

He glanced down at the envelope in his hand. 'It's only a circular,' he said. 'Some central heating firm.' As soon as the words left his lips he knew his mistake.

'We'll have to get some kind of central heating put in before next winter,' Lisa said with energy. 'We must have the house nice and warm for the baby.'

'There are gas-fires in the bedrooms.' He drew a little sighing breath. Even the gas-fires, small and old-fashioned, would be expensive enough to run. And Lisa wasn't by nature given to economy, she seemed to think she had only to express a wish and the means to gratify it would float in on the summer breeze.

'If we sold this house and moved to Cannonbridge,' she

said coaxingly, 'we could buy a lovely new bungalow with central heating already laid on. We could buy one out at Leabarrow, near Carole.' Leabarrow was a newish development on the opposite edge of Cannonbridge.

Derek gave her a despairing look. 'Ivydene isn't ours to sell. Half of it belongs to Janet.' As Lisa well knew.

'I'm positive you could do something about that if you tried, if you went to see a solicitor. Carole says people can always get round that sort of thing if they really want to.' Her tone now held a strong suggestion of a whine and her delicate eyebrows came together in a frown. 'It's so boring being stuck out here in the middle of nowhere.'

'There's no question of selling the house if Janet's against it,' he said. 'And you know she's against it.' Lisa had put forward the suggestion some weeks ago and Janet had abruptly dismissed the notion.

'Carole says we can force a sale, whatever Janet says, and split the proceeds.'

'I'm sure that can't be right,' he said sharply. 'We'd have to reach agreement with Janet on any course of action.' He closed his eyes; half the proceeds of the sale of Ivydene would be nowhere near enough to buy one of the Leabarrow bungalows and he was in no position to raise or finance a mortgage.

He opened his eyes and his expression was once more easy and amiable. 'You haven't read Carole's letter,' he reminded Lisa.

She gave a moody shrug. 'It won't be anything important, it'll just be to say when she wants me to go over there.' She ripped open the envelope and drew out a single sheet covered with a few lines of bold scrawl.

Carole Gardiner was the wife of a welder on an oil rig; they had two small children. The Gardiners had moved to Leabarrow twelve months ago from an industrial town up north. Lisa had met Carole in the waiting-room at her dentist's and they had struck up an immediate friendship.

She glanced over the letter. 'Mike's away again. She wants me to go over there some time this week.' Carole never wanted visitors when her husband was at home, his reappearances were a kind of regular explosive honeymoon. But in Mike's absences she was delighted to have Lisa's company. Lisa usually stayed the night and Carole arranged for a baby-sitter so they could go out for the evening.

'I'll go over there later in the week,' she decided.

'You could go over on Friday morning,' Derek suggested. 'It's the clinic this Friday, you'd have to go into Cannonbridge for that anyway. You could stop over till Saturday.' He never minded these brief absences of Lisa's, they gave him a chance to draw breath, clear his thoughts.

She pouted. 'I've nothing decent to wear.' She gestured at her clothes strewn over the backs of chairs, scattered on top of the chest of drawers. 'Everything's getting so tight round the waist.' It would never occur to her to pick up a needle and scissors, let the garments out. 'I'll be needing a lot of new things soon,' she added. 'And there's all the stuff to buy for the baby.'

She gave him a wheedling smile. 'There's a Mother and Baby fortnight on at Hanson's.' This was the most expensive store in Cannonbridge. 'They have such lovely things. I could go along there with Carole.'

She wouldn't need to fatigue herself penning a reply to Carole's letter, she could phone her from the neighbourhood shop just along the road. She popped in there at least once a day for a tin or something from the frozen food cabinet.

Derek was anxious to steer her away from thoughts of spending. 'Would you like me to run you over to Longmead this evening to see Janet?' he said. 'You could find out if she's coming to stay or not.' They'd already paid a few visits to Rose Cottage although Janet hadn't been very pressing about urging them to come over. 'She may not have had time to write,' he said. 'She must be busy at the end of term. She may just intend to hop on the bus on Friday and come straight over.'

Lisa made no reply. 'We could pop over there about half past seven,' he persisted.

'No, thanks,' she said abruptly. 'I don't see why I should go running after Janet if she can't even be bothered to answer my letters. And anyway,' she added with a return to her childish manner, 'I don't need her now I've got Carole.' Carole was fifteen years older than Lisa and so fitted comfortably into the mother/older-sister slot that Lisa was accustomed to. She much preferred the company of people older than herself, she hadn't kept up with any of her schoolfriends.

And Carole always had plenty of money, was always happy to pay for the steak dinners and wine, tickets for a show, drinks at a club.

'Then if you won't come, I think I'll go over to Longmead on my own,' Derek said. 'I'll ask Janet what she's going to do about the holidays. I'll explain that you're upset she hasn't written—'

'Don't you dare!' Lisa said with force. 'I will not go running after her and I won't have you going running after her either!'

'I don't for one moment think she'd see it like that,' he said mildly. He gave a joking smile. 'Of course she may have more ambitious plans for the holidays, she may be going off on a luxury cruise.'

She could certainly afford it. She'd been teaching for seven years now and she was the type to save. She'd been left some money in her father's will—a sore point with Lisa who'd been left nothing; when her father breathed his last he had no idea that he'd begotten a second child.

Mrs Marshall made her will twelve months before she died and she had divided her estate between her two daughters with scrupulous fairness. The house and its contents were left to them jointly and her investments were split in two, Janet's share to be paid over without delay as she was already of a sensible age, but Lisa's to be withheld till she was twenty-five.

'Promise me you won't go over to Rose Cottage,' Lisa insisted.

He moved his shoulders. 'All right then, if that's what you want.'

She sank back against the pillows with a satisfied air. 'I'm hungry,' she said suddenly, like a child.

'I'll make you some breakfast,' he offered. 'I've plenty of time. What would you like?' He removed the little glass from the tray and set it down on the bedside table.

She put out a finger and touched the rosebud. 'What a pretty colour.' She gave him a delicious dimpled smile and he had a sudden sharp memory of North Africa, the golden idle days, the starry, scented nights. 'I'll have some toast and scrambled eggs,' she said. 'Some of that lime marmalade. And lots of coffee.'

'I'm yours to command, Princess.' He bent down and kissed her, picked up the tray and went briskly down again to the kitchen. The bills were still on the table but he gave them barely a glance as he swept them up into a pile and thrust them back into the drawer of the dresser.

CHAPTER 2

The morning session at Longmead school ended at noon. At five minutes past twelve Janet Marshall walked up Mayfield Lane and pushed open the little wooden gate of Rose Cottage. A trellis brilliant with the full flush of pale pink roses arched over the gate, scenting the air with their delicate perfume. She went up the path to the front door

which was exuberantly garlanded on either side with
great swags of climbing roses, red and white. She took a
key from her shoulder-bag and let herself in.

The cottage was a good two hundred years old; it was
small and set well back from the lane, a situation that
gave it plenty of privacy without making it in any way
isolated. It had a long narrow garden in front and an even
longer strip at the back. The cottage belonged to Oswald
Slater, the owner of Mayfield Farm, and stood upon his
land. It had been allowed to lie empty for many years and
had fallen into sad disrepair, but after the spectacular
rise in property values in recent times Slater had
considered the dwelling worth restoring and modernizing,
and it was now a comfortable little residence with a new
lease of life ahead of it. It suited Janet very well, standing
as it did only a couple of hundred yards from the school.

She hung her bag on a hook just inside the front door.
The tiny hall led into the single living-room which was
simply and pleasantly furnished with pieces she had
brought from Ivydene, pieces she remembered from her
childhood in Ellenborough; they gave her an agreeable
sense of continuity and tranquillity.

She switched on the radio which began to play light
music, but she gave it no more than a fraction of her
attention as she set about preparing her lunch.

She shook out a clean cloth and put it on the table in
the centre of the room. She took out a jug of goat's milk,
butter and cheese from the fridge, reached down a beaker
from the open dresser and brought a tin of crispbread
from the pantry. At the sink she carefully washed a fine
Cos lettuce she had grown in the garden and made it into
a salad with cucumber and tomatoes she had bought on
her Saturday trip into Cannonbridge. All her movements
were quick, neat and methodical.

Before she sat down to eat she crossed to a small desk
that stood against one wall and took out some opened

letters. She began her lunch, looking over the letters again as she ate, frowning as she glanced through them. One letter was untidily written in Lisa's small backward-sloping hand. 'I've been expecting to hear from you,' Lisa wrote. 'To say when you're coming to stay.' To spend a couple of weeks acting as confidante and general dogsbody, Janet thought without enthusiasm; she'd had more than enough of that in her life.

Her father had died when she was ten years old and her mother, never the most independent and strong-minded of women, had immediately cast Janet in the role of man of the family. Her childhood seemed to end overnight. Her mother took to discussing every problem with her — and there was an endless succession of problems; Janet was called on to offer advice, weigh up situations, make decisions.

She sighed and glanced up from the letter and her gaze fell on a picture over the mantelpiece, a landscape, one of half a dozen watercolours on the cottage walls, executed by her father with considerable skill. He had owned and run an artists' supply shop in Ellenborough and had cherished artistic ambitions of his own.

Janet resembled him in appearance, unlike Lisa who took after their mother. Janet was tall and had an exceptionally fine figure, slim and supple. Her head was set with particular grace on a long slender neck; her skin was a delicate olive and her large eyes a clear light hazel. Her naturally curly hair, thick and dark, was cut short and covered her head in close tendrils.

She stood up and took an apple from the bowl on the sideboard, and began to pace about the room as she ate it. She was strongly tempted to let Lisa get on as best she could with the life she had so defiantly chosen for herself. But then again, a young girl in her first pregnancy, no mother to turn to . . . She paused by the table and took a long drink of the delicious goat's milk, creamy and icy

cold. It was difficult to break the habit of shouldering
responsibility, she had acquired the habit so young and
had practised it so long.

After her father's death her mother had put the shop
up for sale, together with the house where they had been
living; the house stood on the outskirts of Ellenborough.
'What would you think of our buying a larger house and
taking in lodgers?' she asked Janet. Mrs Marshall rather
inclined to the idea of businessmen, preferably transients,
with whom it would be possible to preserve some distance.
'I'm not a bad cook,' she added on an increasingly
hopeful note, 'and I know you'd help me all you could.
Do you think we could manage?' After a semi-sleepless
night Janet had decided they could manage and a search
was immediately put in hand for suitable premises near
the business area of Ellenborough.

For the next twelve years Mrs Marshall—with Janet's
unflagging assistance—did succeed in making a living for
the three of them.

Janet worked hard at school—as well as at home—and
did well. Her serious manner and responsible attitudes
suggested teaching as a career and when she was eighteen
she began her training. There was a good college in
Ellenborough and she was able to attend as a day student.
She would much have preferred to live in but there was no
question of that, she couldn't leave her mother to battle
on without her. All during her training she carried the
double load of her studies and her duties at home.
Fortunately she was strong and healthy but by the time
she had finished her training her mother's health, never
very robust, was beginning to fail.

'I've had enough of hard work,' she told Janet. 'And
enough of Ellenborough. I'd like to sell up, go and live in
some quiet, peaceful place and take things easy.' Janet
was delighted at the thought that they might at last be
about to bid goodbye to the long procession of business-

men, and she rather liked the idea of teaching in a
country school.

She found her first post at Stanbourne and as soon as
she was appointed set about finding somewhere for the
three of them to live. 'I know I can leave it entirely to
you,' her mother said with long-justified confidence. 'I'm
sure you'll find a house that will suit us all very well.'

In a short time Janet found Ivydene, a convenient bus-
ride from Stanbourne and close enough to Cannonbridge
for Lisa—at that time eleven years old—to be able to go
in to school there every morning.

The Ellenborough house sold for considerably more
than it took to buy Ivydene and Mrs Marshall invested the
balance on the advice of her bank manager. And as Janet
now had a salary coming in they were able to manage
comfortably without lodgers and Mrs Marshall could at
last put her feet up and take it easy.

A pity she wasn't spared longer to enjoy her leisure,
Janet thought with a sigh; her mother had had a mere
half-dozen years before a stroke took her off.

She picked up another letter and glanced through it,
pursing her lips in thought. It was from Alison Collett, a
friend of hers from the day they'd first met at the age of
five in the playground of the Infants' school at
Ellenborough. They'd sat side by side in the classroom,
had gone on to the same secondary school, trained at the
same college.

Alison had married a couple of years after qualifying
and was no longer teaching. She lived now at Chalford
Bay, an old-fashioned seaside resort some eighty miles
from Cannonbridge. Her husband was a planning officer
with the local authority and they had two small children.

'When are you coming to stay?' Alison asked in her
letter. 'Any time before September will suit us. Just pick
up a phone and tell us what train to meet.' Janet sat for
some moments considering the idea, a good deal more

tempting than a stay at Ivydene with the demanding and capricious Lisa.

She got slowly to her feet, still pondering; she began to clear the table and wash up the lunch things. The radio emitted the time pips and she switched over to hear the news; she rarely bought a paper. As she listened she dried the crockery and put it back on the dresser, then she carefully and neatly wiped over the painted surfaces of the kitchen. When it was all finished to her satisfaction she unlatched a door at the other side of the room and went up the narrow winding staircase to the bedroom.

She opened the wardrobe and looked through the garments hanging from the rail, she pulled out the drawers of a chest and glanced through blouses and sweaters. There were a couple of suitcases on top of the wardrobe and she stood on a chair to reach one down. She dusted the case and took the opportunity to run her duster over the other and also over the top of the wardrobe, then she moved the chair a couple of feet and gave a thorough dusting to the lampshade hanging from the middle of the ceiling. She stepped down again and glanced at her watch—time she was getting back to school. She returned the chair precisely to its place, shook the duster out of the window and went downstairs.

At twenty past one Janet came out of the front door of Rose Cottage and locked it behind her. The voices of the children in the school playground drifted towards her on the slight breeze as she went down the path into the lane.

The lane was very narrow, little used by traffic, barely wide enough for a single vehicle to pass along. The gateway of Rose Cottage offered no access for a car but this didn't bother her; she neither owned a car nor wished to own one.

She went off up the lane at a steady pace. On her left was a pair of semi-detached dwellings, Mayfield Cottages, set close down beside the lane. They were farm cottages, also belonging to Oswald Slater.

There was no one visible in either dwelling but through the open windows she could hear the sound of radios and the clatter of pans and crockery. She walked briskly on to where the lane met the Hayford road.

On the other side of the lane, in the corner made by the lane and the road, stood a small bungalow, Brookside, built between the wars. Over the top of the trim hedge she glimpsed the silvery head of George Pickthorn, the owner of the bungalow, as he stooped over a bed of delphiniums.

At the sound of her step he raised his head and gave her a friendly wave. He was a short, wiry man, fit and active for his years. His face was deeply tanned, with a long pointed nose and a sharp chin; his expression was alert and cheerful.

She exchanged a casual word with him as she turned left into the Hayford road. A few more yards brought her to the gates of the school, a handsome Victorian building of local grey stone, standing on the left of the road.

As she walked up to the front door several children ran up to greet her, bursting with items of news, displaying treasures acquired in the dinner-hour, a curious stone picked up in the playground, a dead butterfly unusually marked. She smiled and answered but kept on her way into the building.

In the front hall the headmaster, Henry Lloyd, was standing beside a little exhibition of international arts and crafts that he'd arranged a few weeks back. He had brought a number of items from home himself and others had been lent by parents and villagers. He was fond of setting up displays of various kinds designed to bring a breath of the wider world into the children's lives.

He was in his middle fifties, very tall and thin with an aureole of fluffy salt-and-pepper hair round a bald crown. He had a quiet manner and his habitual expression was of controlled calm.

On this warm day in late July he wore a tweed suit with a waistcoat, a watch chain draped across the front. His face, his hair, his clothes, were all in shades of sepia, brown and grey; he looked like an engraving in the front of a volume of Victorian sermons.

A boy was standing beside him, asking questions about a piece of jade-green pottery that the headmaster held in both hands, turning it so that the boy could study the elaborate design. The piece was fairly valuable; it had been lent by a parent whose father had brought it back years ago from army service in Malaya.

Lloyd turned and spoke a few words to Janet as she went by to her classroom. He never went home at midday but always took the school dinner-duty himself. His wife was an energetic woman involved in a great many local activities and she had no wish to chop her busy day in two simply in order to cook a meal for her husband. In any case it would have been a problem for him to get home and back in the time. The Lloyds lived at Parkwood, a large late-Georgian house a mile and a half from the school and they had only one car between them which Mrs Lloyd always used to shoot about on her various errands. So all in all it suited Henry very well to eat the school dinner and get on afterwards with paperwork or preparation of lessons.

Janet went on into her classroom. There were only two classes now at Longmead school and she taught the lower. Three or four children were already in the room, reading, drawing, chattering.

There were still some minutes to go before the bell would ring for afternoon school. The first lesson was Nature Study, very popular with the children and one Janet particularly liked herself. She went to a cupboard and took out a box of coloured chalks. She crossed to the blackboard and wrote on it in a beautiful flowing script: British Birds of the Garden and Woodland. The children fell silent, watching in absorbed fascination as she began to draw.

CHAPTER 3

After Janet walked on into the school playground George Pickthorn stood for a moment looking after her. The first time he'd seen her was a few months ago on a bright spring morning as he was coming out of his front door to start work as usual in his garden.

'We're going to have a new teacher,' the children had told him as they stopped to chat over his fence. 'She's going to live at Rose Cottage.' He had heard from other village sources that the new teacher was a good-looking young woman who seemed disposed to keep to herself. But nothing had prepared him for the impact of her appearance as she advanced along the lane towards him on that first morning.

He had lifted his eyes from a rosebush he was pruning and caught sight of that finely moulded face framed by tight classical curls, that proud head and beautiful neck, that tall, marvellous figure. Like the figurehead of a sailing ship, he had thought, and that was how he had seen her ever since.

Now he gave his head a little shake and returned to his gardening. In a day or two he must start painting the neat white fence again, he liked to keep it shiningly immaculate. Tomorrow or the day after he would go into Cannonbridge on the bus—he kept no car—to buy the paint.

He ran a hand along the top of the yew hedge that stood inside the white fence. It felt crisply resilient, thick

and springing under his touch; it was greening up nicely
after last year's careful trimming.

Brookside was a small bungalow but big enough for
George, who was a widower. The bungalow was bounded
at the rear by a field, and on its fourth side by a meadow
that stretched as far as the Cannonbridge road at the top
of the lane. The meadow had not been cut and the green-
gold grass stood tall and plumy in the early afternoon
sunshine.

The brook from which the bungalow took its name was
a sizable stream some four or five feet wide and fairly
deep, murmuring and rippling by, full of trailing weeds
and darting minnows. It ran along the edge of the
meadow beside the lane, through a culvert in the
Brookside garden, and reappeared at the other side of the
Hayford road.

George Pickthorn was sixty-seven years old. He was not
a native of Longmead but had lived in Cannonbridge
until he retired five years ago from his job as a storekeeper
for a firm of electrical wholesalers in the town. He and his
wife had many plans for the years ahead. They had never
had any children; this was always a grief to them but the
marriage was otherwise happy and contented.

Then quite suddenly, without warning, his wife died.
He went up one morning with her cup of tea and found
she was still not awake. She never did wake up. The
hæmorrhage of some microscopic blood vessel in her
brain, the doctor said; it would have been quite peaceful.

That was four years ago. It took him some time to
recover to any extent at all from the shock, the days
slipped by in a grey dream. Then one morning several
weeks later when George opened his eyes, an intention
sprang fully formed into his brain; he would leave
Cannonbridge and go to live in the country.

As soon as he saw Brookside he knew the bungalow
would suit him. 'You're quite sure?' the agent said;

imagining the screeches and caterwauling drifting over from the school, the brickbats and thievings, the general uproar. But George had made up his mind.

Now, on this glorious summer day he was deadheading the roses when the bell rang at the end of afternoon school. The two little girls from Mayfield Cottages stopped as usual to chat to him. Pretty little girls, ten, rising eleven. Jill Bryant with her wide smile and long blonde hair tied back with blue ribbon, and her inseparable friend, Heather Abell from the cottage next door, with her gentle look, soft brown eyes in a heart-shaped face, short black hair cut in a fringe. They were both in the top class, taught by Mr Lloyd.

'My Dad's going to bring me home a kitten soon,' Jill told Mr Pickthorn. Her father worked at Mayfield Farm and Mrs Slater, the farmer's wife, had promised him the pick of the latest litter.

'My mother won't let me have a kitten,' Heather said with stoic acceptance. She was the only child of a widow and accustomed to a certain amount of domestic austerity. He father had worked at the farm until his death a few years ago and her mother still did occasional domestic work in the farmhouse, as well as helping with fruit-picking in the season.

The cottage the Abells lived in was tied, and in the ordinary way Mrs Abell would have had to vacate it when her husband died. But Mrs Slater thought this a harsh practice and pressed her husband to find some alternative. After careful thought Oswald Slater decided that as a replacement for Abell he would in future engage a single man, who could be accommodated in the farmhouse. This would allow Abell's widow and daughter—Heather was at that time five years old—together with Mrs Abell's mother, who lived with them, to stay on in the cottage.

The arrangement worked well. The man who replaced

Abell was a quiet, middle-aged bachelor. He stayed a good four years at Mayfield and gave excellent service; his presence in the farm household was never obtrusive. He left when one of his nephews bought a smallholding twenty miles from Longmead and asked him to go into partnership. Slater had taken on a younger man as his successor.

'I'm going to let Heather share my kitten,' Jill told Mr Pickthorn.

'That's right,' he said approvingly. 'It's good to share.' He took a bag of sweets from his pocket and all three of them dug into the bag with pleasure.

The girls went off a few minutes later with their arms round each other's shoulders. The curve of the lane took them out of George's vision before they reached the cottages.

There was the sound of a vehicle approaching along the Hayford road and George glanced towards the school. Prompt as always at half past four Rachel Lloyd, the headmaster's wife, drove up in her old blue station wagon to collect her husband. As she turned into the playground George gave her his usual wave and Rachel waved back at him in friendly fashion.

This was George's customary signal for tea. He went round to the rear of the bungalow and put down his secateurs and gardening gloves on the seat in the back porch. In this fine sunny weather he liked to come out again for an hour or two in the evening, after he'd cleared away his tea-things and listened to the news.

Inside the school Henry Lloyd heard the station wagon and at once began to lock up. In the classroom next door Janet Marshall also heard the car. She had already finished her own locking up and she came out of her classroom and handed her keys to Mr Lloyd.

'On your way home,' he said, 'I wonder if you'd be kind enough to call in at Mrs Abell's cottage and give her a message from me?' In addition to her other activities Heather's mother acted as school cleaner and caretaker; neither job occupied a great deal of time.

'Yes, of course,' Janet said.

'Ask her if she'll be sure to give the cloakroom a good turn-out this evening.' The headmaster's face looked strained and weary. 'Please don't imply any criticism of her work, she can't be expected to perform miracles in the time she's allowed—but the cloakroom has got rather grubby and it makes a bad impression.'

'I'll be suitably diplomatic,' Janet promised. She went back to her classroom to pick up her things. As she came out of the front door a moment later she gave Mrs Lloyd—sitting waiting in the station wagon—a little wave and spoke a word of greeting. Mrs Lloyd nodded and smiled in reply.

Rachel Lloyd was a large, vigorous-looking woman, a couple of years older than her husband but looking somewhat younger than him. Her thick chestnut hair, lightly streaked with grey, was drawn back into a heavy knot at the nape of her neck; she had the fresh complexion and clear skin of a countrywoman.

Janet walked unhurriedly out of the playground and turned right, in the direction of Rose Cottage. As she passed Brookside she saw that Mr Pickthorn had gone in as usual for his tea. She paused for a moment to admire his delphiniums. They were very fine, a dozen or more delicate shades of blue, a colour she particularly liked in a garden; she must definitely try to grow some at Rose Cottage.

She walked on up the lane and turned in at the gate of the first of the pair of cottages. These were a good deal more modern than Rose Cottage, they had been built shortly after the First World War.

No. 1 was an exact twin of its partner except that it sported a magnificent white jasmine clothing the end wall and a blue ceanothus in full flower in the front garden. The late Mr Abell had been a keen gardener and had taken many prizes at local shows. He had tended the garden up at Mayfield Farm in addition to his duties there as stockman.

The light drifting fragrance of the jasmine greeted Janet as she walked up to the front porch. Mrs Abell's mother, Mrs Perrin, kept a large rocking-chair on the porch in summer, she liked to sit out there knitting on warm afternoons. The chair was empty now, the knitting laid down on the cushions. The front door stood propped open by a large stone and Janet could see Mrs Perrin in the kitchen, standing ironing at the table in the middle of the room. She glanced up at the sound of footsteps and saw Janet coming up the path.

'Do come in, Miss Marshall,' she called out. She was a short, heavily-built woman in her middle sixties with coarse grey hair pulled up into a great bun on top of her head. She was solid and unflappable, healthy and active enough in spite of some trouble with her legs, stout tree-trunk legs encased even in the summer heat in thick stockings, to disguise the veins knotted and corded from years of standing over ironing-boards, cookers, sinks. She more than pulled her weight in the household.

'I expect you want to see my daughter,' she said as Janet stepped across the threshold. The kitchen smelt of warm ironing and ancient horsehair upholstery—from the two huge sagging black armchairs standing one at each side of the hearth. 'She's out in the garden, picking peas.' Mrs Perrin nodded towards the long back garden carefully planted in geometric rows of vegetables, bordered by sternly disciplined bushes and fruit trees. 'Heather's next door, playing with Jill Bryant.'

'I'll go out and speak to Mrs Abell, if I may,' Janet said after a civil enquiry after Mrs Perrin's health. She went out through the kitchen door.

A belt of tall, thickly-grown trees encircled the far end of the two gardens, completely screening them from Rose Cottage. Half way down the garden Janet could see Mrs Abell kneeling among the onions and carrots. She stood up suddenly and darted off to a row of peas, she stooped and began filling her wooden trug with plump young pods.

She was a little scuttling, sideways-glancing woman, colourless and careworn, full of anxieties about life, about managing, averting trouble and disaster. Bad enough when her husband was alive but ten times worse after he fell down dead five years ago from a totally unexpected heart attack among the plant pots and the wooden staging in one of the Mayfield greenhouses.

Janet delivered the headmaster's message and Mrs Abell promised to give particular attention to the cloakroom. As Janet turned to walk back through the garden the two girls, Jill and Heather, came out of the back door of the adjoining cottage and ran down the garden, throwing a ball to each other, laughing and squealing. They caught sight of Janet across the fence and came to a sudden stop.

'Hello, Miss Marshall!' Jill cried and Heather gave her a smile. Janet waved and smiled in reply but said nothing and continued on her way.

Jill's mother, Mrs Bryant, was standing in the back doorway of her cottage. 'You're not to pester Miss Marshall,' she said to the girls in an easy, tolerant tone as soon as Janet had passed out of earshot. 'I'm sure she sees enough of you children during the day, she must be allowed some peace.' She yawned widely. 'I'm going upstairs now for a nap. Don't get up to any mischief and don't go making a lot of noise.'

She went slowly upstairs. On her wedding-day twenty-one years ago Mollie Bryant had been slender and pretty with a fine skin, corn-coloured hair and bright blue eyes.

She'd put on a great deal of weight since then. Her hair had darkened and she'd taken to bleaching it; it was now a harsh brassy colour. Her skin had grown lined and weather-beaten and had developed a permanent shade of light brick from stooping over the oven in her kitchen.

She was fond of cooking and served a substantial high tea every evening when her husband and son came in. Nowadays she felt more and more the need to toil upstairs out of the hot kitchen in the sultry afternoons, put on something loose and cool, lie down and close her eyes. She opened the bedroom door and began to unbutton her dress; five minutes later she was fast asleep.

Shortly before six her husband Ken walked down from Mayfield Farm for his tea. He would go back again afterwards to work in the turkey sheds for an hour or two.

He came through a wicket gate set in the screen of trees and walked up the back garden towards the house. He was a tall, powerfully-built man in his late forties, with straight black hair sleeked back from his forehead and dark bushy eyebrows meeting across his nose. His sleeves were rolled up, showing muscular brown arms with a strong growth of black hair.

The two girls ran up to him, besieging him with questions about the kitten.

'I can't bring it home for another day or two,' he said, laughing as Jill swung on his arm. 'We can't take it from its mother yet—you don't want the poor creature dying on you.'

'No, I suppose not,' Jill said reluctantly. She went with him into the house and Heather ran home next door for her tea.

Ken pushed open the back door and went into the kitchen. Mollie had already come downstairs again, somewhat refreshed after her nap. She hadn't bothered to comb her hair or powder her face—she wasn't going anywhere and she wasn't expecting visitors. She had

merely slipped on a cotton kimono and thrust her bare
and unlovely feet into a pair of flat mules.

She had laid the table and was now busy cutting bread.
'You're back then,' she said to her husband in ritual
greeting, looking up at him with a cheerful smile.

He gave her a nod, mastering his irritation at her
slatternly appearance. He had to discipline himself these
days not to snap at her. He'd tried friendly suggestion,
diplomatic hints, outright advice that she should lose
weight, do something about her hair, her skin, her
clothes. He still felt it not impossible that out of that slack
flesh, the lines and folds, the slim nymph of twenty-one
years ago might somehow be conjured up again.

But none of his efforts produced the slightest effect.
'I'm not a girl any more,' Mollie said with easy
acceptance. 'Can't expect to stay young and beautiful for
ever.'

Ken made a stern effort now to speak amiably to her as
he went over to the sink to scrub his hands. 'Warm old
day,' he said. 'We'll end up with a storm if this keeps on.'

'I wouldn't mind a drop of rain.' She began to butter
the bread. 'It'd cool things down.'

He studied her reflection in the mirror above the sink.
The kimono was gaily coloured with a jazzy design in
lemon, apricot and orange. Mollie had always had a
fondness for bright colours and they'd suited her well
enough when she was a girl. She had bought the kimono
on holiday a couple of years ago to wear on the beach,
now it was downgraded to housewear in hot weather. The
belt kept slipping and the kimono fell apart periodically
to reveal a dingy nylon petticoat straining across her
bosom before she clutched the folds about her again and
refastened the belt. He dried his hands on the roller
towel, closing his eyes briefly against a glimpse of vast
bare thighs, quilted and dimpled, pale as lard.

The roar of a motor-bike sounded in the lane, growing

louder as Dave Bryant drove up to the cottage, dying away again as he parked the machine at the side of the house. He came in through the back door a couple of minutes later, carrying his crash helmet under his arm.

'Hello, Mum, Dad.' He grinned at Jill. He was a sturdy lad of twenty, nothing special in the way of looks, a frank, intelligent face and a generally likeable air, the kind of lad an employer would probably engage on sight.

He was apprenticed to a Cannonbridge firm of builders on a day-release scheme, working three days a week for the firm and spending the other two days at the local technical college. He was an industrious lad and a good student, he had taken more than one prize.

'Sit down, everyone!' Mrs Bryant commanded. She patted her frizzed hair into place and began to dish up. They all ate with keen appetite, there was never any trouble with finicky eaters at Mollie's table.

'This is a very good rhubarb tart,' Dave said with keen appreciation towards the end of the meal. He and Jill never regarded their mother with criticism, they took her as she was, not having known her in her willow-slim, corn-gold days.

'I'll bake you a couple of tarts for the party on Friday if you like,' Mrs Bryant offered expansively. The party was an end-of-term social at Dave's college and she'd already promised half a dozen goodies.

'Oh yes, please,' he said with enthusiasm. 'That'd be great.'

'Are you inviting Clive to the party?' Jill asked her brother.

'I did ask him,' Dave said without much interest, 'but I don't think he'll come. He said he'd let me know.'

'You should try to persuade him,' Mrs Bryant said as she stood up to fetch a massive fruit cake from the larder. 'He never goes anywhere, he sticks in those digs all the time, making his models—it can't be healthy for a lad of his age.'

Clive Egan was twenty-one years old, the only surviving child of Mrs Bryant's cousin. His parents were dead and he lived in lodgings in Stanbourne with a Mrs Turnbull, an elderly widow. He was employed as a general building worker by the Cannonbridge firm where Dave Bryant was apprenticed.

'It would do Clive good to go to the party,' Mrs Bryant said with a jerk of her head. 'It's not much of a life, living in digs.' She poured herself another cup of tea. 'Mrs Turnbull's a good sort but the lad needs more life at his age.'

Ken took a huge slice of cake and bit into it. It was undeniably excellent, full of plump raisins and glacé cherries. His mood softened. 'Go on, Dave,' he said. 'You ask Clive again. You'll find he'll go to the party with a bit of persuading.'

CHAPTER 4

Five miles away, in the village of Stanbourne, Clive Egan and his landlady were about to begin supper. Clive had been working in Stanbourne for the past ten days, assisting with a central heating installation in one of the large houses. He was a tall, heavily built young man with broad shoulders and strongly muscled arms. His fair hair was clipped close to his head, his eyes were a deep clear gold with a restless darting gaze.

'I expect you've nearly finished on that heating job,' Mrs Turnbull said as they sat down to cold bacon-and-egg pie and salad. She was a perky little woman with quick neat movements and sharp brown eyes; her thin grey hair was dragged back into a scanty bun.

'Another couple of days should do it,' Clive said. 'Then I'll be working over at Longmead, a roof repair and guttering job.'

She glanced up. 'Oh—if you're going to be over Longmead way, perhaps you wouldn't mind calling in at Mayfield Farm for me, ordering a turkey from Mrs Slater.' Her oldest sister and her husband were celebrating their golden wedding early in August and Mrs Turnbull had promised a turkey for the family reunion dinner.

'Yes, sure,' Clive said. 'That won't be any trouble.' He helped himself to potato salad. 'I can walk up to the farm in my dinner-hour.'

'I shall want a good big bird.' She inclined her head, considering. 'Be sure to explain to Mrs Slater about the dinner, tell her it must be a top-quality bird, I don't mind paying. And ask her if they still deliver or if I'll have to arrange to have it fetched.'

Supper had already been eaten at Parkwood, the Lloyds' elegant late-Georgian house on the edge of Longmead village. Rather a meagre supper; it hadn't taken the Lloyds long to despatch it.

Rachel didn't feel called on to provide much in the way of an evening meal during the week in term-time. Henry could eat as much as he wanted in school at midday and in the course of her own driving hither and yon about the neighbourhood in execution of her many duties she was usually given a sustaining succession of cups of tea and coffee, home-baked cakes and cookies, slices of pies and quiches.

Not that Henry was disposed to be critical of his supper. He had little appetite nowadays, had grown steadily thinner over the last few years and scarcely noticed any more what was set before him.

When the supper things had been cleared away Rachel

fetched her embroidery basket and settled down in an easy chair in the sitting-room with the radio tuned in to a concert of classical music. There was no television set at Parkwood. 'I've never felt the need of one,' Rachel said when anyone commented. Her parents would have been horrified at the idea of introducing such a time-waster into the household and she had never seen good reason to depart from their attitudes and strictures. Parkwood had belonged to her parents and she had lived there with them before she married Henry fourteen years ago.

In his bachelor days Henry had been accustomed to television. He had lived with his widowed sister in a snug little house in Cannonbridge and they had watched many an entertaining or instructive programme together in the placid evenings.

They had led an agreeable, uneventful life that flowed steadily on and seemed as if it would continue in the same tranquil way forever. Henry was at that time deputy head of a Cannonbridge primary school with good hopes of a headship somewhere before long.

And then one February evening his sister, engaged in a little dressmaking, providing herself with a pretty new blouse for the spring, went upstairs to fit the blouse in front of the long mirror in her bedroom. Some alteration in the way the garment hung upon her caused her to frown, some difficulty in getting a good fit over one breast, but she pushed the little anxiety to the back of her mind, went downstairs again with resolute cheerfulness and altered a dart in the bodice. Eighteen months later she was dead.

The snug little house had belonged to her and on her death it passed to her son, a professional man, married with a young family, living in Scotland. 'We don't relish the thought of uprooting you,' he told Henry at the funeral, 'putting you to inconvenience, but—'

The snug little house must be sold and Henry must

provide himself with somewhere else to live.

In the course of his many visits to the hospital during the last six months of his sister's life, Henry had become acquainted with Rachel, who was an active member of the Friends of Cannonbridge Infirmary.

She befriended Henry and was very good to him in those bleak and difficult days. She was energetic, formidably competent and strong at a time when he felt he lacked all those qualities himself and so was particularly disposed to admire them in others.

Rachel soon discovered that he was hoping to find a headship as well as somewhere to live. She knew that the headship of the village school at Longmead would fall vacant within the next year and she also knew that the governors were hoping to find a candidate who wouldn't need to live in the headmaster's house attached to the school. It was a dwelling of no great size and the governors wanted to incorporate it into the school to provide some badly-needed extra facilities.

It was a hopeful and expansive time then, in the village as well as in the nation at large. Longmead seemed poised on the brink of growth, there was talk of a light industrial estate being built, a garage and a filling-station, new houses and shops.

The notion that Henry should apply for the Longmead headship soon insinuated itself into the air between himself and Rachel and at very much the same time another idea also found its way into the atmosphere—that they should marry.

The headship wasn't precisely what Henry had in mind. 'But it will do very well as a stepping-stone,' Rachel pointed out and he was inclined to agree. He was also aware that an energetic and competent spouse, well bred and well heeled, would be no drawback on the road to higher things. He applied for the headship and became engaged to Rachel in the same month.

At the time of his marriage Rachel's parents were old and frail and Rachel informed Henry in a tone of authority that they couldn't be expected to live much longer. She was their only child. 'Parkwood will come to me,' she assured him. So also would the antique furniture, the pictures and objets d'art, together with the substantial investments on which her parents lived. After the old couple had dutifully passed on Henry would in due course be able to apply for a better headship elsewhere; the house was readily saleable and would fetch an excellent price.

But things hadn't worked out quite like that—

Henry's thoughts were suddenly interrupted as Rachel glanced up from her embroidery and said, 'By the way, I've got a very good corn dolly for you, I was given it this afternoon. It will go admirably in your little craft exhibition.' She had spent the afternoon with an arthritic village woman who had to be driven into Cannonbridge twice a week for treatment. The woman had been clearing out a cupboard and had come across an elaborate dolly she'd made some years ago, before the disease attacked her fingers; she knew Mrs Lloyd was interested in such things.

Rachel passed the dolly across to Henry without glancing at him; she scarcely ever looked at him directly. He wondered sometimes if she had any real notion of what he looked like, if she had ever seen him properly and fully, even at their first meeting in the hospital corridor.

He took the dolly and looked at it, turning it over to study it. Beautiful, intricate workmanship; ancient, mysterious pattern.

'Do thank her for me,' he said. 'The children will be most interested.' All his exchanges with Rachel were touched on Henry's part with formality and courtesy. No expression altered the set of his features as he spoke to her. He had learned over the last few years to keep his face calm and still at all times and as a result it was unusually free from lines without looking in any way youthful.

He crossed the room and put the dolly where he would remember to take it to school next morning. He paused by the window and glanced out at the soft blue sky. 'I think I might do an hour or two in the garden,' he said as he had said on a great many other fine evenings.

Rachel made no reply, absorbed again in the music and in her stitching; she was embroidering a set of kneelers for the church. She took great care over the work, knowing it would stand as a measure of her skill for years to come. Henry wondered if he had actually spoken, she gave no sign of having heard. He experienced again the curious unpleasant feeling that had begun to afflict him of late, that inside the precincts of Parkwood he no longer existed, that if he were to pause to look in the hall mirror he wouldn't be able to see his face. A thought that terrified him sometimes when he woke in the night was that he might soon begin to find he was ceasing to exist in other places as well, and might end up before long not existing anywhere at all.

He left the room and Rachel scarcely noticed that he'd gone.

He went up the graceful curving staircase to his bedroom across the wide landing from his wife's room. He changed into an old pair of trousers and a superannuated shirt and went downstairs again and out through a side door into the garden.

The air was warm and dry. A few feet from the door a great bed of cream and pink spiræas flaunted its full splendour but he gave it only a passing glance. He went over to the toolshed and selected a billhook, then he walked with his head lowered down to the far end of the garden, overgrown and midgy, full of birdsong and humming green shadows.

He began to lay about him with ferocity, slashing at the grassy tussocks and the long arms of brambles, laying low the great strong flowering weeds, putting paid to the offending growths for the time being, if not unfortunately finishing them off for ever.

The evening air was still warm and caressing when Janet Marshall came out of the back door of her cottage and walked up to Mayfield Farm for her goat's milk. She bought the milk as she needed it, usually three or four times a week.

Facing her as she walked up the field was the end wall of the turkey sheds which had been constructed some years ago from existing farm buildings. The sheds formed three sides of a rectangle, the open side facing across the field to the back of the school. She could hear the clatter from inside the sheds and as she drew nearer, the raucous cries of the birds.

Ken Bryant, her next-door neighbour from Mayfield Cottages, came out of the rear of the main farm buildings some little distance ahead on the right and walked down the field towards her, on his way home.

He glanced over and saw Miss Marshall with her lithe, slender figure, her beautifully shaped head covered in close curls. How neat and trim she looked in her casual outfit of jeans and check shirt. He closed his eyes for a moment in a brief shudder at the thought of his wife in a similar rig.

He raised a hand and called out to Miss Marshall. She halted and stood waiting till he came up to her. 'I wanted to have a word with you about Jill,' he said. His dark eyes showed open admiration.

'Yes?' She gave him back a courteous, neutral glance. A strong growth of black hair showed at the open neck of his shirt. He gave off a powerfully masculine farm odour—by no means disagreeable—that no amount of baths or changes of linen could ever totally remove.

Ken was ambitious for his children and he was currently anxious about his daughter's maths. 'She'll be going to the Cannonbridge Comprehensive in September, as you know,' he said, 'and I'm afraid her maths are going to let her down. I shouldn't like her to get off to a bad start.' He'd be grateful if Miss Marshall would agree to coach Jill in the holidays. 'You'll be here for some part of the time, I'm sure,' he added. 'Of course I'll pay whatever's right and I'd see she wasn't a nuisance to you.'

'Jill's not in my class,' Janet pointed out.

'I know that but I don't like to ask Mr Lloyd, he's got a lot on his plate. And Parkwood's a good mile and a half away, it wouldn't be anywhere near as handy for Jill. I'm sure Mr Lloyd wouldn't mind you coaching her.' He saw her hesitate. 'Think about it,' he urged. 'You've no need to give me an answer right away, I'll mention it to you again later.' He went off down to his cottage, whistling.

As Janet passed the open front of the turkey sheds the young resident farmworker, Neil Fleming, came out of one of the sheds. He'd already changed out of his white overalls and was shrugging on a drill jacket.

'Hello there!' He gave her a friendly smile. He'd given her the eye, bowled over by her looks, when she first came to Longmead back in the spring, not many months after his own arrival at Mayfield, but it had taken him very little time to realize she wasn't interested.

He walked with her towards the dairy on his way to the farmhouse. 'I've got quite fond of goat's milk myself since I've been here,' he told her with a grin. 'I'd never drunk it before, never fancied it. I always thought it'd have a rank taste but now I'd sooner have it than cow's milk.'

He was a pleasant-looking lad with a fresh open face, curling sandy hair and a thickly freckled skin. He had a very full lower lip and his grin showed a milk tooth surviving in the front of his mouth. It gave him a touching, boyish air. He was twenty-five years old, studying and saving in the hope of getting into farm management; he felt there was precious little chance of ever owning a place himself.

He went on through the rear entrance of the farm-house, a large old dwelling of mixed period and considerable charm, while Janet turned aside into the dairy, fresh and cool, lined with white tiles.

Mrs Slater was standing by a window, carefully setting a shallow pan of milk down on a slabbed surface. She glanced briefly up as Janet came in and gave her a friendly nod, then she gently settled the pan into place. She straightened up and wiped her hands on a towel. She drew a long breath and moved her shoulders, easing them.

She was a small slim woman in her middle thirties with a clear, fine skin and short light brown hair simply cut. Her lips were curved in a faint habitual smile and her customary look was one of amiable reserve. Over her freshly laundered dress of flowered cotton she wore a white overall with the sleeves rolled up, showing her pretty arms, smooth and rounded, with delicately tanned skin.

'It's the end of term on Friday, isn't it?' she said as she poured the milk for Janet. 'I'm sure you're looking forward to the holidays, it must be tiring dealing with youngsters all the time.' The Slaters had no children. 'Have you made up your mind yet if you're going away?' She stood chatting for a few minutes.

Margaret Slater wasn't a native of Longmead, she came from Stanbourne. After eighteen years of marriage she was still looked on by the village — and still looked on herself — as an incomer. Not that anyone in Longmead disliked or resented her but she wasn't Longmead born and bred and never could be.

She had come to Mayfield Farm as a girl of sixteen,

when Oswald Slater's mother was still alive. The old lady had begun to ail and had been ordered goat's milk by her doctor. 'I've been thinking of getting someone to live in, to give me a hand with the housework and cooking,' she told Oswald. 'If I can find a sensible girl who also knows something about livestock, we could buy a goat and she could look after it as well as helping in the house.'

Within a short time she found Margaret, neat, capable and well-mannered, the daughter of a Stanbourne smallholder. Margaret had kept goats since she was eight, and regularly took prizes at shows. She also reared turkeys and was doing well with them on a small scale.

Twelve months later old Mrs Slater died and shortly afterwards Oswald asked Margaret to marry him. She was hard-working, easy to get on with and accustomed by now to Mayfield ways. Above all she was there. No need for him to go to all the trouble of putting on his best clothes and embarking on the long and tedious business of running round the countryside trying to locate a suitable bride.

Oswald was thirty-seven at the time of his mother's death and had never had much time or inclination for courting. He was a powerfully built man of medium height, with large hands and little small talk.

He consulted Margaret's parents before speaking to the girl and they in turn had a long chat with their daughter when she rode over on her bicycle for tea the following Sunday afternoon. It was agreed all round that it would be a fine match for her. She was happy to agree, she liked living at Mayfield and saw her future there as peaceful and secure. The marriage was settled and took place without delay.

Shortly afterwards Margaret suggested that she might introduce turkey-breeding to Mayfield and Oswald was rather taken with the idea. 'But I'll have to go into the costs,' he said cautiously. The costs proved reasonable and he approved the plan which Margaret promptly put into operation, overseeing the whole enterprise and subsequently managing it; it had prospered well, expanding over the years.

Now she wiped over the surface of the table as Janet picked up her milk. 'You're not going away yourself?' Janet asked her.

Mrs Slater shook her head. She'd never been brought up to holidays, had never formed the habit and certainly never felt the need. And Oswald Slater wasn't a man to encourage such flighty notions.

'I wouldn't know what to do with all that free time,' she said with her little smile. 'And what about my goats? I couldn't leave them to someone else to look after.'

As Janet walked down the field back to her cottage she glanced over at the school. The window of the head-master's office overlooked the field but the building was empty now. Mrs Abell had finished her cleaning and locked up for the night.

I think I'll put in an hour on the vegetable patch, Janet decided as she opened the wicket gate leading into her garden. The ground had been long neglected when she came to Rose Cottage but she'd wasted no time in getting to work on it. Now there were lettuces and peas to pick, radishes to thin out, scarlet runners to inspect. There was still a fair-sized stretch to clear and dig, as well as the regular chores of weeding and hoeing, but they were all tasks she enjoyed.

She let herself in at the back door. Flickering shafts of sunlight strayed into the living-room through the branches of an apple tree, there was a light pervasive scent of roses. She hummed a tune as she put the goat's milk away in the fridge.

CHAPTER 5

Early on Friday morning, when the horizon was streaked with rose and gold, the first blackbird uttered a soft whistle in the Brookside garden, followed a moment later by a missel thrush. In his narrow bed George Pickthorn heard the sounds in his sleep and smiled with pleasure. In his dream he was running over the common—the old common, the common of his childhood—with his little Jack Russell terrier, dead these sixty years. Some part of George's waking adult mind leaned into the dream and formulated the thought: I could get a little dog, a Jack Russell, no reason why I shouldn't have one now, why didn't I think of it before? I'll start looking out for one right away.

Along the lane at Rose Cottage, Janet Marshall lay sound asleep in her little bedroom, dreaming she was shut tight inside a box. Outside the box something breathed and panted, trying to get in at her, scratching and tearing at the wooden sides, but she felt no fear, knowing herself safe and snug in her stout little nest.

A mile and a half away, in the best bedroom at Parkwood, Rachel Lloyd lay at ease in the large double bed that had been her parents'. She wore a faint smile on her dreaming face. She was skimming along the fields and hedgerows of the village like a bird, soaring up over the church into the cloudless blue, looking down on the houses and farms spread out below.

Across the landing in the second-best bedroom Henry woke, as always these days, thirty seconds after the first bird uttered its morning note. He had been trying to make his way through a dense black wreathing fog but his feet and legs were weighed down, his arms heavy and powerless.

He came fully awake. Friday, his brain registered, the last day of term. He stared up at the ceiling with its ornate mouldings. How many more terms would he see? Year by year the school roll fell relentlessly. Fourteen years ago there had been three teachers, now there were two.

It was only a matter of time before Longmead went the way of other village schools and closed its doors for the last time. He had no illusions about what that would mean for him. It would be almost impossible at his age to get another teaching job of any kind, let alone a headship.

And in any case Rachel wouldn't dream of moving away from Longmead. He believed now that she'd never had any such intention, she had merely allowed him to believe she had.

Her parents hadn't obligingly departed this life as early as he'd been led to expect. They had lingered on into ripe old age and year by year the city headship had receded. It was ten years after the marriage before Rachel's father died and her mother had finally closed her eyes only twelve months ago; by then it was far too late, the dream was over. All he'd amounted to was the head of a dwindling school in a little village.

He viewed with horror the thought of continuing to live in Longmead after the school finally closed. One by one all the other services and functions of the village would wither and die, Longmead would slide into stagnation and decay.

The rosy visions of expansion had come to nothing, there was no industrial estate, no blossoming of new houses. Already the parish had been amalgamated with that of Stanbourne, there was no resident vicar now at Longmead.

At one time when Henry thought of retirement he had looked forward to it as an exciting, fertile time of life. He saw himself active and energetic, speaking at conferences, lecturing to interested groups up and down the country, writing on educational matters for the national press, being interviewed on television and radio. Now he knew he would simply be stranded here in this tiny backwater, isolated, growing old; nobody would give a damn what he thought about anything.

It was a struggle every morning now to rouse himself to tackle the day's work. He dreaded to think what his state would be when there was no longer even that regular stimulus to spur him up out of the dark pit.

He threw back the covers and got out of bed, thrust his feet into slippers. When he and Rachel returned from their honeymoon Rachel had firmly indicated that at Parkwood they would occupy separate rooms. 'In case Mother needs attention in the night,' she told him. 'It will mean less disturbance for you.' Now, as he went silently down the wide staircase, he was deeply thankful that he had his own room and could wander about when restlessness woke him, could read or listen to the radio.

After the honeymoon he and Rachel had never again gone away on holiday together. There were always her parents who couldn't be left; until last year there had still been Mother. From time to time Rachel went off to stay with one or other of her cousins and Henry occasionally visited a nephew or niece.

He went into the kitchen and made himself some tea. He drew back the curtains and stared out at the soft dewy morning. He drank his tea, scarcely tasting it, then he went upstairs again, back to his own little territory. He switched on the radio, adjusting the volume so as not to disturb Rachel in her bower across the landing. He got back into bed to listen to precise tones bringing him news of other people's disasters from all over the globe.

At seven o'clock he was able to rise officially and half an hour later he joined his wife at breakfast. Rachel was a stickler for punctuality—in herself as well as in others; she regarded it as a sign of sound moral fibre. She was a great believer in fibre, in the backbone as well as in the diet.

She was already dressed for the day in one of her reliable and useful beige summer outfits, relieved by touches of white. She wasn't much interested in clothes and had long ago adopted a manner of dressing that saved a great deal of time, thought and money, and always sent her out looking trim and feeling comfortable: tweed suits from September, navy and white from April, beige and white from June. She bought good clothes and looked after them; they lasted indefinitely and never went out of style. She regarded the whole of the vast international fashion industry, reared up on vanity and an insatiable thirst for novelty, with powerful contempt.

'There's a letter from Aunt Miriam,' she said as she placed a pot of instant coffee on the table. 'She wants us to take her over some things.' Aunt Miriam, the youngest sister of Rachel's mother, lived alone in a cottage at Ribbenhall, a village ten miles the other side of Ellenborough. She was at present in hospital in Ellenborough, suffering from an attack of shingles.

'We can go over there tomorrow afternoon,' Henry said. He reached for the packet of muesli and shook a little into his bowl.

'I'm having the Finch boy again this afternoon.' Rachel was communing with herself rather than with her husband. 'I shall pick him up at twelve-thirty. His mother has to go into Cannonbridge, to the Social Security office.' The Finch boy was a Mongol, the son of a woman who was herself of less than normal intelligence. Rachel often had the child for an hour or two while his mother performed some essential errand.

Henry made a vague murmur in reply and dug at his

muesli without appetite.

Rachel poured the coffee. 'I hope Aunt Miriam's recovered before I go away,' she said with a frown. 'But of course if she is still in hospital, you'll be free to go over and visit her, now the school holidays are starting.' This year there was neither Father nor Mother to prevent them going away together and there had been a time earlier in the summer when Henry had feared that at long last he might be compelled to accompany Rachel to some watering-place.

But by great good fortune Aunt Miriam, until a few weeks ago hale and hearty, had suddenly begun to crumble at the edges. She was immediately instated in the void left by the death of Rachel's mother, and was now officially the relative who must always be able to summon one or other of them in an emergency. With luck she might survive to hold down the post for another ten years.

So Rachel was off next week to stay with a cousin in Devon and Henry had arranged to visit his nephew in Scotland late in August, after Rachel got back.

She took a piece of dark rye bread from a foil-covered packet. She bought it at a delicatessen in Cannonbridge; the bread was heavy, dense and sour, but she believed it did wonders for her internal economy. 'I must get on,' she said briskly. 'I have a great deal to get through today.' She began with great energy to cover the piece of bread with butter and honey.

The front bedroom of Ivydene was full of dancing points of light stealing in over the top of the curtains—not yet drawn back for the day. Lisa Schofield opened her eyes, stretched and yawned aloud. She was alone in the big bed, Derek must have gone downstairs to make the tea.

She reached for a cigarette and glanced at the bedside clock, saw with surprise that it was a quarter to nine. Derek must surely have gone off to work by now—and without bringing her her tea.

She gave a sound of irritation, then she saw his clothes neatly folded over the back of a chair—so he was still in the house.

She heard the sounds of a tray approaching, footsteps on the landing and a moment or two later Derek came into the room. His dressing-gown was pulled tight round him and he had a scarf tucked in at the neck. He looked flushed and tired.

'I'm afraid I've got one of my throats,' he said in a hoarse thick voice. He approached the bed and set down the tray on the table. 'I'd better not kiss you.' He suffered intermittently from something he called a strep throat. He didn't consult a doctor for it, he gargled, sucked lozenges, stayed huddled into himself for a day or two, then struggled about till he felt normal again.

Lisa gave him an anxious look. It was no part of Derek's duties to assume the role of patient. She was off to Carole Gardiner's this morning and wasn't planning to return till tomorrow afternoon or evening. She very much hoped she wasn't expected to cancel her jaunt.

'I shan't go into work today,' Derek said. 'I should be all right by Monday. When you get to Cannonbridge, would you mind ringing the firm and explaining?' Cannonbridge Mail Order were well used to Derek's throats.

'You're sure you'll be all right?' Lisa could safely express concern now she knew she wouldn't have to stay at home.

'Yes, of course.' He climbed back into bed, still in his dressing-gown. 'I'll sleep most of the time. I won't need anything except hot drinks and I can go down and make one when I want it.' He grinned reassuringly at her and then shivered violently. 'Don't worry about me, I'm as tough as old boots.'

*

After morning break Janet Marshall took the girls of both classes for a Nature walk while Mr Lloyd and the boys tidied the school garden for the holidays. She led the girls out through the front gates and turned left along the Hayford road. A few minutes later they crossed the road and took a footpath that struck across the fields.

Perched high on the roof of a detached house a little further along the road, Clive Egan stared down at the trio heading the little procession, Miss Marshall with the two girls one on either side of her, long blonde hair on the left, tied back with blue ribbon, short dark bob on the right.

'Pass over the slate rip,' the tiler called across to him. Clive blinked away his thoughts and passed him the tool.

It was past noon when Rachel Lloyd came out of the front door of Parkwood and locked it behind her. The old blue station wagon was already drawn up in the drive. She glanced up at the house as she walked across to the vehicle, checking that all was in order, the windows closed against intruders or sudden violent rainstorms.

She looked fresh and cool in a well-tailored dress and jacket of beige linen with a white trim on the collar and pockets. She had dabbed her face and hands with a few refreshing drops of English lavender water, a perfume she held superior to any other, the only perfume her mother had ever used, the only perfume suitable for a woman of breeding and refinement.

She reached the car and got in. Five minutes to allow for hold-ups, twenty minutes to drive through the village and out the other side to Prior's Hill, where Barry Finch lived. Yes, she was in nice time; she couldn't abide being late for anything but at the same time resented being too early, wasting valuable minutes that might be far more usefully spent in setting to rights the affairs of others.

She was quite fond of Barry Finch. He was four years old and of a happy, smiling disposition that always seemed to spread calm and content around him. His mother — Mrs by courtesy rather than by any right of law — was a youngish woman who had lived alone since the death of her mother some years ago. She had never been very sure how Barry had come into existence but she suffered no local censure on that account; the village was only too thankful that Barry hadn't been followed by a string of equally unaccountable brothers and sisters.

Rachel drove out on to the road. It was a hot, sultry day. 'I'm sure there's thunder in the air,' she had told Henry at breakfast. Not that thunder bothered her, she wasn't a foolish ninny to develop migraine or crouch terrified under the stairs when lightning crackled across the sky.

She was very content. She had now all she had ever wanted from life. Good health, a comfortable income, independence, a handsome house, the knowledge that she was respected — even admired — in the local community; sufficient power, influence and time to carry out her aims. A husband with his own occupation and absorptions, who never troubled or incommoded her, compliant in the matter of where and how they should live, a man to whose career she didn't have to play second fiddle.

She had often congratulated herself on her shrewd judgment in pouncing on Henry when he showed his face above cover. He was in every way an eminently suitable lay-figure in her full and satisfying life.

She had never wanted children. One of the reasons she had left it so long before casting about for a suitable mate was this determination to have nothing to do with motherhood — or as far as possible with the indelicate preliminaries of motherhood. A matter in which Henry, thank goodness, had proved accommodating.

She found the position of married woman highly satisfactory, so superior even in these unstructured days to that of a spinster daughter, and more particularly so in the countryside, where old ideas lingered on; it gave a woman status and a certain blend of freedom and respectability that was most agreeable.

As she drove up the rise where a path led off to the church she turned her head and glanced across to where here parents lay. The churchyard was neat and well kept, like a picture-postcard, with its yews and cypresses dark and massy against a vast blue sky, the gravestones glittering in the brilliant sunlight. She must pop along there tomorrow with fresh flowers. So gratifying to know one had been a devoted daughter, to be able to lay down one's head at night in the tranquillizing knowledge of duty well done and a total absence of any necessity for the faintest whisper of self-reproach.

She drove through the village, acknowledging nods and waves here and there, and out on to the Prior's Hill road. She loved the village and all the countryside around, so green and lush. 'So very English,' she was fond of saying. Brown-and-white cows knee-deep in meadows shaded by clumps of tall spreading trees; lacy white weeds flowering along the hedgerows. To live in such a place, to know one would always live there, what more could anyone ask?

She put her foot down and the car rose like a bird up the long slope of Prior's Hill. Mrs Finch was standing at her cottage gate, watching out for her, with Barry standing beside her. When he saw the car he jumped up and down with pleasure, laughing, waving both hands, his rosy cheeks plump and freshly scrubbed, his dark eyes sparkling with glee.

Rachel halted by the gate. 'I'll just pop inside and fetch Barry's things,' Mrs Finch said as Rachel stepped from the car. 'I won't be a moment.' She had an air of earnest simple endeavour. Barry stood smiling at Rachel with delight, lifting his face up to her with love and trust.

Mrs Finch came back down the path with a sweater and a box of toys. With her narrow foxy face and lank light brown hair cut in a straggling fringe, she looked as if she had stepped out of a Saxon wood. 'I'll bring Barry back by four o'clock,' Rachel told her, speaking slowly and clearly. 'You'll be home by then.'

Mrs Finch handed over the sweater and toys. 'I'm going on the bus,' she said, proud of her ability to negotiate such hazards alone.

'Do you know the time the bus goes?' Rachel asked.

Mrs Finch's eyes clouded and she looked up at the burning sky.

'Five to,' Rachel told her. 'You're in good time, you've no need to go running in this heat.'

Mrs Finch smiled in relief. She bent and kissed Barry. 'I'll bring you something nice back from town,' she promised. 'If you're a good boy.'

'Barry's always a good boy when he's with me,' Rachel assured her. She settled him firmly into his seat and fastened the seat-belt. She glanced at Mrs Finch's festive summery outfit. 'You must take your umbrella,' she told her with authority. 'We may have a storm, I can feel it in the air.'

'Oh no,' Mrs Finch protested. 'It's so lovely and sunny.' She knew she looked her best; she wore her prettiest short-sleeved dress of sprigged cotton and the straw hat with fruit on it that she'd bought at the last village jumble sale. She smelled powerfully and arrestingly of some perfume that she'd found discarded—with good reason—behind a bench in the waiting-room at the bus station on her last trip to Cannonbridge. She didn't want to spoil the effect of all this finery by carrying her old black umbrella.

'Take your umbrella,' Rachel repeated slowly and patiently. 'We're sure to have a storm before evening. If it comes this afternoon you'll be soaked to the skin.' She switched on the ignition and Barry looked joyfully out at his mother, waving furiously with both hands. Rachel leaned across as she prepared to move off. 'Now do what I say,' she called through the open window. 'Take your umbrella. I'm never wrong about these things.'

CHAPTER 6

At dinner-time Clive Egan ate his sandwiches in the toolshed of the house where he was working. The tiler cycled off to the Mare and Colt to wash down his bread and cheese with a glass of ale.

Clive didn't mind a solitary lunch, he always had a book — and his thoughts — for company. At half past one he shook the crumbs out for the birds and packed away his sandwich box in his duffel bag. He glanced at his watch. Just nice time to walk up to Mayfield Farm and deliver his landlady's message.

He set off up the road at a good pace. The air was still and heavy, the birds sang in a muted key, the sunlight had a dull, brassy quality. He reached the farm and walked round to the rear buildings.

The midday meal was eaten early at Mayfield and Mrs Slater was already back at work in her little office near the turkey sheds. She made a note of Mrs Turnbull's order. Certainly she could deliver the turkey and she could promise a superb bird, one that would do full justice to the golden wedding dinner.

She stood in the doorway chatting to Clive; she had known his parents and she always enjoyed a chat with anyone from Stanbourne. She enquired about his job, how things were working out for him. He answered in monosyllables, looking down at the ground, giving her an occasional sidelong glance.

Oswald Slater came striding down to the office. He looked more thick-set than ever these days, his brown hair was beginning to grey. He frowned as he walked along, slashing vaguely about with a stick, absorbed in his thoughts. He looked up and saw the two of them standing in the doorway.

'Oh—young Egan,' he said, and gave him a nod. 'I got on to Jessup,' he told his wife. 'I'm going over to see him this afternoon when I've finished at the dentist.' His dental appointment was for four-thirty. He'd just heard that Jessup—a farmer over at the other side of Cannonbridge—was selling up and moving south. 'I'll see what he's got to sell, there may be something I can use—if the price is right.'

'Will you be home to supper?' his wife asked.

'Yes, I should be back before seven. Half-six or so.' He looked at his watch. 'I'll leave here at a quarter past four, that'll give me enough time.' He was always concerned to save time, energy and money.

'That house you're working on,' he said to Clive. 'It needs repointing.' He hated to see good property deteriorate for want of a few pounds spent at the right time.

Clive raised his shoulders. 'We're just doing the roof and spouting. No one's said anything about pointing.' Slater made him feel vaguely uneasy, any middle-aged man with a forceful manner made him feel uneasy. 'I'd better be getting back,' he said.

In the garden at Brookside George Pickthorn was already at work again on his fence. He was anxious to finish it by this evening. Next week he must make a start on the construction of a small summerhouse.

The afternoon's work went well, without interruption. Shortly before half past three, just as he was thinking it was about time for the mothers to start turning up at the school to collect the youngest children, he heard a loud crashing sound from the direction of the crossroads at the top of the lane.

He halted in his painting. The sounds died away. He set down his brush and pot of paint and swiftly wiped his hands on a rag. He came out of his garden and set off up the lane at a rapid pace.

As he passed the first Mayfield cottage he saw old Mrs Perrin walking stiffly down the path towards him. Her abandoned chair rocked on the porch.

'Been an accident, I should think,' she called out.

He gave her a brief nod. 'I'm going to see if I can do anything.'

There was the sound of approaching wheels, the mail van coming towards him on its afternoon round. It slowed as the postman, Tom Spencer, caught sight of George. The van halted and Tom stuck his head out of the window.

'Lorry shed its load,' he called out. He jerked his head back at the crossroads. 'No one hurt.'

'I was going along to see —'

'No need. The driver's got a lad with him, he's phoning the police from the Mare and Colt.' He grimaced. 'Carrying a load of metal castings. I'd just got clear of the crossroads, I was emptying the box at the top of the lane. He was coming too fast, tried to turn, the load couldn't have been properly secured.'

'I'll get back to my painting then,' George said.

'Hang on, you can take this with you. I was going to drop it in.' Tom handed over a gardening catalogue in a brown-paper wrapper.

George stood aside to let the van go on its way. He tore the wrapper from the catalogue and began to glance through it as he walked back down the lane.

He didn't need to stop and tell Mrs Perrin what had happened, Tom Spencer had halted by her gate and was retailing the news.

George edged past the van. One or two mothers were assembling now in the school playground and he waved to them as he went into his garden. He was strongly tempted to go on indoors and sit down with his catalogue but duty called him. He put the catalogue inside the back porch and returned resolutely to his task.

Inside the school the air was full of the sense of summer holidays about to begin. Posters and charts were taken down from the walls, vases emptied, nature tables cleared of collections of grasses, leaves and flowers, caterpillars in matchboxes, dead moths and butterflies. The subdued clatter was punctuated by the intermittent droning of a saw in the adjoining field where the two Mayfield farmworkers were repairing and extending fencing.

In the school hall the craft exhibition was dismantled, the more robust items being handed over to children to return to parents but fragile or valuable exhibits were put on one side to be returned by the headmaster.

All the top class children were leaving to go to the Cannonbridge Comprehensive in September, most with feelings of pleasure, some with apprehension and regret. They had clubbed together to buy farewell presents for the two teachers and presented them after the final hymn and prayers; a pair of stout gardening gloves for the headmaster, a box of embroidered handkerchiefs for Miss Marshall. Some of the girls shed tears. One or two had brought little gifts of their own for Janet, a bottle of toilet water, a pretty string of beads. Heather and Jill had joined together to buy her a silky headscarf patterned with wild flowers.

The two girls were laden as they went out through the front door of the school, their satchels and shoulder-bags stuffed with belongings cleared out of desks and lockers, treasures bestowed, gifts exchanged.

As they reached the school gate Heather looked up the road to her left and saw Clive Egan walking towards them carrying his bag of tools.

'There's Clive,' she said to Jill. 'He must have finished early.'

'Oh good!' Jill said. 'I can ask him if he's going to the party at the Tech tonight. Dave wants to know.'

She put the question to him as soon as he came up. He merely shook his head in reply and she left it at that.

'I've forgotten my skipping-rope,' Heather said suddenly. 'Wait for me, I'll go in and get it.' She went back inside the building.

The school was empty now of children. Heather went into her classroom and found the rope in her desk; she managed to force it into her satchel. As she was leaving again she glanced in at the other classroom and saw that Miss Marshall had almost finished clearing up. A bulging duffel bag and canvas holdall stood by the door but a number of items still waited on the table. Miss Marshall was gazing down at them with a frown, wondering how she was going to get them home.

'There's a basket in the hall,' Heather said. 'From the exhibition. I'm sure Mr Lloyd would let you borrow it.'

'Clever girl!' Janet smiled at her. 'I'll go and ask him.'

He was in his office, occupying himself while waiting for his wife by clearing the shelves by the window.

'Yes, of course, borrow the basket by all means,' he said. He looked out at the sky. 'Those clouds are starting to build up. I think we're in for a storm.' In the field the two farmworkers hammered in fencing-posts.

When Janet got back to her classroom Heather was going round the room picking up the last scraps of litter and putting them in the waste basket. Under a desk she came across a red and yellow ball.

'This belongs to Stuart Hitchman,' she said, holding it up. 'Shall I take it and give it to him?'

'No, I'll take it,' Janet said. Stuart's father was the licensee of the Mare and Colt and Janet wanted a word with him about the boy's increasing sleepiness in class, his inability to concentrate—due in Janet's opinion to being allowed to stay up far too late in surroundings that were much too stimulating for a young boy. Parents could be tricky animals, touchy and sensitive about their young. A discreet, pleasant word now, casually given while handing over the ball, and there would be the whole of the summer holidays for irritation and resentment to drain away.

She came out of the school with Heather a minute or two later. The playground was empty now except for Jill standing by the gate chattering to Clive who stood listening in silence, gazing down at his feet.

Janet looked at him as she came up. 'I know you, surely,' she said. 'You're from Stanbourne.' Her memory threw up a name. 'It's Clive Egan, isn't it?'

'That's right.' His face turned a dull red.

'You came to the Stanbourne school one day, to mend a broken window.' He gave a nod and his face turned an even deeper red.

'Shall I carry your things?' he asked suddenly.

'No, thanks, it's all right, I can manage. I haven't far to go, just up the lane, next door to the girls.' She started to walk in the direction of Rose Cottage and he fell in beside her. She asked him about his work, what job he was doing in Longmead, and he began to answer with more animation.

George Pickthorn watched the little party approach. He was busy now on the last stretch of fence; if he came out earlier than usual after tea he would just about finish it before supper. The girls called out to him as they went by, not stopping to chat today on account of their loads.

In the front garden of the first Mayfield cottage Mrs Abell stood trapped beside a flowerbed with a trowel in

her hand. She'd come out to do a quick tidy-up of the
beds and borders but Mrs Bryant from next door had
popped out five minutes later for a breath of air. She'd
spotted Mrs Abell and at once walked over to the fence, in
the mood for a nice little chat.

Mrs Abell had no time for little chats and no taste for
gossip but she couldn't be rude, not living next door, it
didn't pay. She couldn't maintain her minuscule part in
the conversation while crouching over the begonias so she
had to stand up, idle and fuming, nodding and smiling,
saying, Well I never, and I dare say.

Heather caught sight of her mother. 'Can I go and play
with Jill's kitten?' she called out.

'Yes, all right,' Mrs Abell called back. 'But don't be
late for tea.' She nodded a greeting at Miss Marshall and
the Egan lad, then she seized the opportunity to make her
escape indoors, darting past her mother placidly knitting
and rocking on the porch.

Mrs Bryant, robbed of her captive listener, was
compelled to make do with whoever else was at hand. She
called out a comment to Janet on the oppressive heat but
Janet merely gave her a polite smile and word of reply and
went on to Rose Cottage. Mrs Bryant then bent her
attention on Clive, asking him if he'd decided to go to the
party after all. He shook his head and she began trying to
persuade him. He made no response but stood with his
eyes lowered.

The two girls ran into the cottage and set down their
burdens. They came running out again a couple of
minutes later to show Clive the kitten, a pretty little black
and white creature with a pink satin ribbon tied round its
neck in a lopsided bow.

Mrs Bryant continued her exhortations to Clive. He
still didn't look at her but stood stroking the kitten with a
forefinger.

'I'm hungry,' Jill said suddenly to her mother. 'Is there

anything to eat?'

'I'll find you something,' she said. 'What about you, Clive? Would you like a piece of cake? Or a drink of squash?'

He shook his head. 'No, thanks. Mrs Turnbull will have my supper ready.' He began to walk off with his head still lowered.

Mrs Bryant stood looking after him, shaking her head in mild irritation. 'Come on then,' she said to the girls and they followed her into the house, still crooning over the kitten.

The kitchen was stiflingly hot in spite of the open window; a couple of fruit tarts for supper were baking in the oven. Mrs Bryant went to the larder and took some buns from a tin. 'These'll have to do you for now,' she said. 'You don't want to spoil your supper.' She picked up a newspaper and stood vigorously fanning herself with it. 'I'm going to sit outside on the porch for a while. What are you two going to do?'

'We're going in the shed,' Jill told her. Her father had let her have the old toolshed outside the back door for a Wendy house; he'd built himself another shed, larger and stouter, at the end of the garden. 'Heather's going to help me fix up a place for the kitten,' she added. She'd got a lovely little cat basket fitted with a cushion, she'd bought it with her pocket-money at the last jumble sale. 'We're going to make a new cover for the cushion.' Heather's mother had given them an old summer dress to cut up; the material had a pretty pattern of birds in flight.

'I suppose it's all right about the birds,' Heather said anxiously. She wasn't sure of the effect the pattern might have on the kitten's developing psyche.

'Of course it'll be all right,' Jill assured her. 'I should think it'll make him kind to birds when he grows up, then he won't get into trouble for killing them in other people's gardens.' She was sure Miss Marshall wouldn't be at all

pleased if he went springing over the flower beds at Rose
Cottage leaving bloody carcases in his wake.

Prompt at half past four George Pickthorn heard the
sound of Mrs Lloyd's station wagon approaching the
school. He looked up from his painting to give her a wave,
then he carried his tin and brush round to the back
porch, went inside to wash his hands and put the kettle on
for tea.

Mrs Bryant's eyes were closed and her head had slipped to
one side when the oven timer emitted a loud ring. She sat
up with a start and went into the house. She opened the
oven door and saw with relief that the tarts were done;
now she could go upstairs and slip her dress off, have a
proper lie-down.
    As she crossed the kitchen to pick up the oven cloth the
two girls came out of the shed and closed the door behind
them; Jill was holding the kitten. They saw her through
the kitchen window and at once halted, they stood
giggling and whispering together. She guessed what they
were up to, she rapped on the glass and gestured them
sharply inside the house.
    'You're not to go bothering Miss Marshall,' she said.
'Taking the kitten round to show her.' She stooped to take
a tart from the oven and the blast of hot air struck her full
in the face. She straightened up, gasping, and set the tart
down on top of the stove. 'She's seen enough of you all
term, do at least let her have her holidays in peace.' She
blew out a long breath and took out the second tart,
beautifully golden, with a crisp sugared top. She nodded
in satisfaction and set the tarts down to cool by the
window.
    'I'm off for a nap now,' she said as she restored the oven
cloth to its hook. 'Don't go making a lot of noise, I've got a
bit of a headache. I've had it all day, I reckon it's the

heat.' She glanced at the clock. Five minutes past five. Plenty of time for a snooze, with luck she might get rid of the headache altogether.

CHAPTER 7

The accident at Mayfield crossroads had now been dealt with. The road was clear again, the warning signs removed, the lorry gone on its way. Constable Drew glanced about, making sure everything was in order. Sergeant Goddard was already in the car, leaning back with his eyes closed, thinking about a very long, very cold drink.

As the constable made an entry in his notebook he heard a bus approaching along the Cannonbridge road and the sound of someone running up the Mayfield lane. He glanced round and saw a lad—a young man— running up the lane towards him with a toolbag under his arm.

The bus halted a few yards past the crossroads; the driver had seen the lad and was holding the vehicle. The lad ran past the constable with barely a glance, his face flushed in the heat. He reached the bus and sprang aboard. As the vehicle roared on its way the church clock struck a quarter past five.

Constable Drew went over to the police car. 'We can get off now,' he said. The sergeant made no reply, merely opening his eyes with a look of intense boredom.

The constable got into the car and started the engine, he was going to drop the sergeant at his house on the Hayford road before continuing into Cannonbridge. He turned the car down the Mayfield lane to cut through to the Hayford road.

A short distance along the lane he saw on his left two

little girls coming down the path of the first dwelling, a cottage set well back from the road. Pretty children, one with long flaxen hair tied back with a blue ribbon, the other with short dark hair cut in a fringe. The blonde girl was carrying a black and white kitten with a pink satin bow at its neck.

The girls reached the open cottage gate and stood waiting for the car to pass. An arch of pale pink roses curved over the gateway. Like a birthday card, Constable Drew thought with fleeting sentimentality, the children, the kitten, the roses.

He recognized the girls, not by name, but he'd given a road safety talk at Longmead school a few weeks back and he remembered the pair sitting together in the top class, the blonde one very bright, asking intelligent questions. He slowed the car to a halt.

'Finished school then?' he asked with a grin.

Jill nodded. 'I remember you,' she said. 'You talked to us at school.' She smiled. 'This is my new kitten.' She held it out for him to see.

'Very nice,' he said. 'Looks a healthy specimen.'

'We brought it to show Miss Marshall.' Jill jerked her head back at the cottage. 'This is where she lives. But we were too late, she's gone off on her holidays.'

In the passenger seat Sergeant Goddard opened his mouth in a vast yawn. 'Be sure to close the gate behind you,' he said.

Jill gave an emphatic nod. 'Oh yes, we'll do that.'

Constable Drew remembered Miss Marshall. Not an easy lady to forget. Handsome as a Greek statue, wonderful figure—and a manner that made it plain no games were being played here today.

'My Dad got the kitten from Mrs Slater up at the farm,' Jill said, stroking the silky fur.

Sergeant Goddard made a restless movement and glanced openly at his watch. 'Is that so?' Constable Drew said to Jill. He deliberately went on chatting for a little longer. The sergeant was his junior by a good ten years, he needn't think that in all places and at all times he was indisputably cock of the walk.

'Your Miss Marshall's going to have warm enough weather for her holidays,' the constable said to the girls with resolute affability. 'Unless it all breaks up in a storm. And that wouldn't surprise me.' He set the car in motion at last with a farewell smile and wave.

And it did begin to storm later in the evening. Great banks of dark cloud built up over Cannonbridge, the sky grew black, brilliant branched lightning flared above the trees, rain lashed the fields.

Next morning the air was cool and fresh but this welcome effect lasted only a few hours. It was starting to warm up again in the afternoon when Henry Lloyd drove his wife over to Ellenborough, taking with them the things for Aunt Miriam in hospital. It was a little warmer on Monday when George Pickthorn went into Cannonbridge to buy the wood for his summerhouse, and warmer still on Tuesday when he began to saw it.

The sun was growing daily stronger when Rachel Lloyd went off to visit her cousin in Devon. In the tranquil windless afternoons George Pickthorn sat in his garden wearing a panama hat, reading and dozing. It had grown hot and sultry again when Mrs Slater delivered a mammoth turkey to Mrs Turnbull's sister. The bird was eaten with appreciation and sustained praise at the highly successful golden wedding dinner two days later.

The roses arching over the gate of Rose Cottage were fully blown when Tom Spencer stopped his van one morning to drop a letter in. A week later when he called again with a parcel of books the petals were lying in pink drifts under the gate.

He walked up the path to the front door and rang the bell. There was no reply. He wasn't surprised, the place had an empty, shuttered look. Birds sang from the tall belt of trees and there was a loud buzz of insects. A hatch of blowflies, his mind registered.

Better leave the parcel somewhere safe, round the back. He went round and knocked at the back door, expecting—and getting—no response. The buzzing was very much louder now, probably a dead bird in the garden.

He tried the back door, just possible it wasn't secured and he'd be able to slip the parcel inside the little porch. But the door resisted him.

What about the shed? He glanced over at it, an open-fronted wooden structure with its back to the fence. No, he couldn't leave the parcel there, anyone coming round to the rear of the cottage could see inside it, could just reach in and filch the books. Better call next door and leave the parcel there.

He made to walk off again along the path but then paused and stood frowning down at the stones edging the border. The buzzing was surely very loud indeed. He walked all round the cottage, trying to peer in at the windows but net curtains obscured his vision and there were longer, heavier curtains too, half drawn. He could make out very little.

The buzzing was loudest at the back of the house, it definitely came from inside and not from the garden. He stood irresolute for a moment and then suddenly made up his mind and went rapidly off next door.

Mrs Bryant answered his ring, half shielding herself behind the door. She was not yet dressed for the day, she wore an old housecoat and ancient slippers.

'Yes?' She stuck her head and shoulders out at an unnatural angle. The dingy once-apricot nylon of her housecoat was all snagged and pilled. In his time Tom Spencer had seen many morning ladies peering out at odd angles from behind doors and he was certainly no stranger to Mrs Bryant's deshabille. He held up the parcel.

'Is Miss Marshall away?' he asked.

'Yes, she's over at her sister's in Hadleigh, I believe. Do you want to leave that? I'll see she gets it when she comes back.' She put a hand round the door.

'I was wondering if you had a key to Rose Cottage.' He didn't part with the books.

Her scanty brows came together. 'A key? No, I haven't.' She stared up at the sky. 'I think there's a spare key up at the farm.' She flashed him a sharp look. 'Why do you want it? I don't know that Miss Marshall would care for someone going into the cottage while she's away.' She stretched her hand out further, revealing a few more inches of grubby nylon. 'I'll take the parcel, it'll come to no harm.'

He still retained his hold on the books. 'It's the noise,' he said, hesitant and yet reluctant to forget the whole thing, hand over the books and go on his way. He'd seen one or two things in his time, he couldn't shake off a certain unease.

'Noise?' Mrs Bryant forgot herself and flung open the door. 'What noise?'

'Like blowflies. From inside the cottage, round the back. I think she must have left some food out, forgot it when she shut the place up. I wouldn't like her to get back from her holidays and find the place—' He didn't have to spell it out, not to a countrywoman.

'No indeed!' she said with fervour. 'Look, don't you worry about it, you leave it to me, I'll see to it. I'll mention it to Ken at dinner-time, he can get the key from the farm and we can pop in and take a look round, we'll soon clear up anything that's wrong.'

He hesitated. 'I'd just as soon it was seen to now.' The feeling in his bones, he couldn't bring himself just to climb into his van and drive off.

She shrugged. 'Oh well, if you're set on it. Ken's working in the field back there.' She jerked her head. 'I'll get Jill to run up and ask him to fetch the key.'

She went back inside the house and out through the kitchen to the shed by the back door where Jill and Heather were trying to fit a bonnet that Heather had knitted, on to the head of the protesting kitten. A few moments later the two girls came out of the shed and ran down the back garden and out through the wicket gate.

Tom Spencer went back down the path to wait by his van. The moment he'd gone Mrs Bryant ran upstairs to her bedroom with a speed that would have astonished the Women's Institute. She tore off her housecoat, sending buttons popping unheeded about the room. She kicked off her slippers, gasped and struggled into a summer dress with a startling pattern of cherry-red and white. She thrust on her good sandals, fluffed a powder puff over her face and tugged a comb through the top layer of her frizzed hair.

The girls came flying back into the house with two keys on a length of string. 'They're for the porch and the back door,' Jill said breathlessly.

Mrs Bryant went out to the van with the girls following at her heels. Tom Spencer took the keys, briefly registering the sudden marked alteration in Mrs Bryant's appearance. He went round to the back of the cottage with the trio close behind him.

'Oh, my word, I do see what you mean,' Mrs Bryant exclaimed as the buzzing reached her ears. 'It certainly does sound like blowflies. There must be a terrific great swarm of them.'

Tom unlocked the outer door. 'I shouldn't come in,' he said to Mrs Bryant. 'And I shouldn't let the girls come in either.' He gave her a single forceful glance.

A couple of dozen large blowflies darted about inside the porch, stirred to frenzy by his entry. He closed the door behind him and unlocked the inner door. He stepped inside, into a swirling roaring black flight, banging and sweeping into his face.

A dreadful stench rose up at him. He pulled out a handkerchief and clapped it to his nose. He went on into the living-room and looked about.

A bottle of squash, one-third full and with the cap lying beside it, stood on the draining-board with a glass next to it; both bottle and glass were choked with flies. On a table near the window an assortment of articles lay beside a duffel bag and a canvas holdall. He glanced inside the bags but there was nothing amiss, just books and papers, a miscellany of school articles.

An ironing board stood against the wall with a neat pile of ironing placed on it, a blue chintz curtain folded on top. He crossed the room and looked in at the walk-in larder. No open food, nothing untoward. He stepped back into the living-room.

The loudest buzzing seemed to be centred on the stairs. He went over to the door that shut off the staircase; the door was secured by an old-fashioned latch.

Very cautiously and with a horrible feeling of nausea he lifted the latch; the door opened towards him. A dense cloud of blowflies swept frantically out, billowing into his face. The stench was overpowering.

There was no window in the stairwell, only the daylight coming in over his shoulder. The steps broadened as they rose, to take the curve of the stairs. On the broadest step, halfway up, under a blue chintz curtain, lay what the summer and the blowflies had left of Miss Marshall.

CHAPTER 8

It fell to the lot of Derek Schofield to carry out the identification of the body. In a bureau drawer at Rose Cottage the police came across a bundle of Janet Marshall's private papers, neatly arranged, and among them a letter from Lisa Schofield written a few weeks back, complaining that Janet hadn't let her know her holiday plans.

Mrs Bryant had some slight acquaintance with Mrs Schofield. 'I spoke to her one Sunday afternoon when she was over here visiting with her husband,' she told Chief Inspector Kelsey. 'She's very young, she looked hardly old enough to have left school.' Mrs Bryant looked up at the Chief, a big solidly-built man with a head of springing red hair and large craggy features. 'And I do know she's expecting a baby,' she added.

I can hardly ask her to identify the body, Kelsey thought. He passed a hand over his big fleshy nose. Judging by the letter, Lisa Schofield seemed an emotional, somewhat childish young woman, not a breed the Chief was particularly fond of. In his eyes the first and most important service any human creature could render his fellows was to grow up, and until that had been accomplished he remained in varying degrees a pain in the neck.

Monday morning, he pondered, the husband was pretty certain to be at his place of work. Ken Bryant was able to supply the information that Schofield worked at the Cannonbridge Mail Order Company. Ken had spoken to Schofield when he first drove over to Longmead, had shown him where he could park his car in the run-in by the old quarry workings beyond the school.

Kelsey went off to Cannonbridge without delay to speak to Schofield. The mail order firm was housed in an old warehouse near the railway station and had a somewhat run-down and cheerless air. Kelsey spoke first to the manager, a sharp-eyed man with a deeply lined forehead and pursed-up lips as if he were habitually in receipt of worrying news.

'I don't know how Schofield's going to take this,' he said when the Chief had indicated his errand. 'I should think he's got enough on his plate already.' He shook his head. 'He's only been married a few monhts. Came to me wanting promotion if you please, or at the very least a rise in salary. Didn't get it, of course,' he added with gloomy relish. 'We're hanging on here by the skin of our teeth.' He grimaced. 'Not that Schofield would ever be executive material.'

'You pay his salary into his bank, I imagine?' Kelsey said.

The manager was brought up short by the abrupt change of tack. 'Well, yes, we do,' he said after a moment.

'I'd like the name of the bank.' The Chief offered no explanation. The manager supplied the information and a junior was despatched to fetch Schofield from his desk in Accounts. The Chief wouldn't sit down while he waited but remained standing by the desk, immobile and silent, his head inclined at a listening angle. The manager needed little encouragement to rattle on and kept up a ceaseless flow.

It seemed that Schofield was no more than a clerk. 'He moved into his wife's house when he got married,' the manager said in a tone compounded of envy and malice. 'Just as well, I should think, they'd have had a long wait if he'd had to buy a house himself. And you never saw such a dreary old place as he was living in before he got married—just the one room, and a poky little room at that. I called round there once when he was off sick with one of his throats.' He gave a short laugh. 'I couldn't exactly see Lisa living there. I don't suppose he even let her clap eyes on the place.'

'Lisa?' Kelsey echoed. 'Are you acquainted with Mrs Schofield?'

The manager looked surprised. 'I should say I am. We all know Lisa, she worked here till she was married. She was here a couple of years, she came straight from school.'

Old lusts and resentments sparkled his eyes. 'She made a dead set at Schofield the moment she got through the door. God knows what she saw in him. We'd all got him down as a permanent bachelor, he never had a girl-friend, never went anywhere.' He gave the Chief a significant glance. 'We did rather wonder about him sometimes. Then all at once, this pretty young girl, all over him. He couldn't believe his luck.' He pulled a face. 'Of course, there's the other side of it. Pretty young girls, they've got expensive tastes.'

There was the sound of approaching footsteps. 'I'll talk to Schofield alone,' Kelsey said.

The manager got to his feet with reluctance. He'd been looking forward with keen expectation to watching Schofield's face as the news was broken; he'd also looked forward to hearing a few more details about the death.

For totally different reasons the Chief was also anxious to observe the look on Schofield's face but the expression when it did appear was more a series of swiftly succeeding flashes of emotion.

Schofield seemed at first totally unable to take in what the Chief was telling him. Bewilderment, incredulity, protest, passed in turn across his face. When he did at length digest the fact that his sister-in-law had been found dead in circumstances that established beyond doubt that she had met a violent end two or three weeks ago, horror and revulsion spread open and naked across his features.

He got to his feet and went unsteadily over to the window. He flung it open and stood hanging over the sill with his eyes closed, gulping in great trembling breaths of warm air laced with dust and traffic fumes.

At last he drew back into the room. He was deathly pale. 'I'm sorry, I can't believe it.' He put a hand up to his face and collapsed into the manager's chair.

'Lisa—she'll be—' He looked for a moment as if he were about to suggest that the news should be kept from his wife and then the folly of the notion seemed to strike him. 'No, of course not. She's got to know.'

'I'm afraid I must ask you to identify the body,' Kelsey said and a look of even greater horror spread over Schofield's face.

'Oh no,' he said in hopeless protest.

'I'm afraid there's no alternative—unless you know of some other relative?'

Schofield shook his head. 'Only some distant cousins up north somewhere.'

'We can't very well ask your wife.'

'No, of course not.' Schofield looked up at him with a terrified air. 'It'll have to be me, I see that.'

All at once he began to cry. He put an arm across his face like a boy in a playground shielding himself from blows, the tears soaked into the sleeve of his jacket.

He stopped as suddenly as he'd begun, he took out a handkerchief and dried his eyes.

'I'm sorry about that,' he said with an effort at briskness. He rose suddenly to his feet. 'I'd like to get it over with.' He thrust the handkerchief back into his pocket and held himself rigidly upright.

'I'll have another word with the manager,' Kelsey said. 'You'll hardly be coming back in here again today, your wife's going to need you.' He intended to postpone his own visit to Ivydene till after they'd got the results of the post mortem, give Madame Schofield time to digest the news. He had no wish to assist at a display of hysterics.

'Yes, of course.' Schofield, still braced, gave a quick nod. He crossed to the door and held it open for Kelsey to pass through.

'I got to the Mayfield crossroads just before three-thirty,' Constable Drew said. 'Sergeant Goddard came by at a quarter to five. He was getting a lift home but he dropped off to give me a hand. We were there till just after five-fifteen. No vehicle went up or down Mayfield lane the whole time I was there.'

'Any pedestrians?' Kelsey asked.

'No one went down the lane towards Rose Cottage. A couple of mothers with children — from the school — came up the lane towards me, not long after I got there. That would be at about a quarter to four. And there was a young builder lad, carrying a toolbag.'

'Clive Egan,' Kelsey said.

'He came running up the lane and got on the bus just as we were leaving.'

'Running?' Kelsey echoed sharply.

'He had to run to get the bus, he almost missed it.'

Kelsey's features relaxed somewhat. 'Could someone have darted across the lane from one field to the other without your seeing him? Or even gone up or down the lane, just slipped past behind your back? You could hardly have been looking down the lane the whole time.'

Drew made a stubborn movement of his shoulders. A stubborn man altogether, in the Chief's opinion, not always the most desirable trait when it came to establishing hard fact, however desirable in other aspects of police work.

'I'd have noticed,' Drew said. A countryman born and bred — as he was fond of telling listeners — though stationed now in Cannonbridge for many a year, he'd have seen movement in a country lane behind his back in the dead of night with his eyes blindfolded. Or was convinced he would. The Chief didn't share his conviction.

'When you stopped by the gate of Rose Cottage to talk to the girls,' he said, 'did you see anything unusual? Hear anything? Notice anything at all? Anything in any way unusual?'

Drew shook his head. 'But she could still have been alive at that time—even though the girls got no answer when they knocked at the door.'

Kelsey pressed the tips of his fingers together. The girls had told him they'd knocked for some little time, unwilling to accept that Miss Marshall wasn't in. They'd gone round to the back of the cottage and knocked there as well, but they hadn't peeped in at any of the windows. Kelsey had pressed them hard on that point, assuring them he would think no less of their good manners if they admitted peeping in, but he couldn't shake them.

'He could have had his hand over her mouth when the girls knocked,' Drew suggested. 'He could have stayed frozen like that till they went away.' The girls had heard no sound from inside.

'Or she could have been unconscious,' Kelsey said. 'Knocked out or fainted, she could have been killed some time later.'

Janet Elizabeth Marshall, spinster, 29 years old, of Rose Cottage, Longmead. Kelsey sat at a table in the kitchen of the village hall, looking down at the newly-opened file. On the table were three photographs of Janet as she had been in life.

The first was a school photograph taken in the middle of the summer term, Miss Marshall standing at one end of the group and at the other end the headmaster, Henry

Lloyd, with his hands linked behind his back, his tall thin figure held stiffly upright, his look that of a man much given to thinking.

The other two photographs were holiday snapshots taken some years ago, they were among a number in a folder in Miss Marshall's bureau. One showed her as a schoolgirl sitting on a holiday beach between a little fair-haired girl and a middle-aged woman frowning against the sun. In the second snapshot Miss Marshall, now a young woman, stood with two other girls of about the same age as herself, in the dappled sunlight of an avenue of trees. A large building of classic lines was visible in the background; one of the girls held an armful of books.

Kelsey studied the photographs. He found it impossible to associate the lovely smiling girl in them with the object he had seen on the staircase at Rose Cottage.

Equally difficult to credit that such a fine-looking young woman had not had plenty of men friends. But Mrs Bryant seemed certain she had not, certainly no fiancé or lover. 'Not she!' she'd said at once, loudly and with emphasis. 'For all she was so handsome.' She had then burst into heavy shaking sobs.

One good female friend at least Janet appeared to have had; they had found a letter from the friend lying unopened on the doormat. It was from a Mrs Alison Collett in Chalford Bay, postmarked ten days ago, wondering why she hadn't heard from Janet about her proposed visit, asking her to try to get over during August as the Colletts were going away themselves in September.

It certainly looked as if Janet had intended going somewhere; a partly filled suitcase lay upstairs in the bedroom. She had last collected her goat's milk from Mayfield Farm on the Wednesday evening before term ended, telling Mrs Slater that she still hadn't finally made up her mind about her holiday plans, she might or might not be calling in again for milk.

Kelsey sat in thought, drumming his fingers on the table. It seemed highly likely that she'd been killed on the Friday term ended, shortly after she came in from school. She was wearing the same clothes she'd worn at school that day, she'd poured herself a drink of squash but hadn't had time to put the bottle away again. She'd begun unpacking the bags she'd brought with her from school; she hadn't started any preparations for a meal.

He glanced at his watch. Half past one. In a couple of hours they'd have the results of the post mortem. He pushed back his chair and stood up. Two or three people in the village he'd better have another word with before going into Cannonbridge.

At the other side of the door there was a subdued hum of voices. The usual comings and goings, a steady trickle of folk with something to tell, something to hazard, spite or gossip or speculation to unload. And, somewhere amongst it all, tiny diamond points of invaluable fact.

He pushed open the door and went into the hall.

An elderly woman with a stout body enveloped in voluminous folds of floral cotton was sitting talking to Detective-Sergeant Lambert with an air of profound importance. Lambert glanced briefly up at Kelsey, swiftly assessing the Chief's mood and intentions.

Kelsey made a gesture indicating that neither Lambert nor the elderly lady should pay any attention to him. He prowled briefly about the room, chewing the inside of his cheek, pausing to study a map of the area drawn on a blackboard set up on an easel.

'Miss Marshall never stayed to school dinner,' the elderly woman told Sergeant Lambert. 'She always went back to Rose Cottage.' The woman, together with one of the mothers, served the dinners and washed up afterwards. No cooking was done at the school, the meal was brought in containers from the central kitchen in Cannonbridge.

As Kelsey strode towards the exit he gave the sergeant an abstracted nod. A word first with George Pickthorn at Brookside, then a visit to Mayfield Farm, and possibly, if time allowed, another call at Mayfield Cottages.

CHAPTER 9

Forty-five miles away in Ellenborough, the afternoon heat shimmered above the concrete of the hospital forecourt as Henry Lloyd came down the steps and made his way to the station wagon. He carried two suitcases and had a carrier bag tucked under one arm. He stowed the bags away in the car and went back inside the hospital to collect Aunt Miriam from the entrance hall.

She was sitting huddled in an easy chair, clutching her handbag on her lap; she looked very old and very frail. He put a hand under her elbow and steered her to the door; she swayed a little as they negotiated the steps.

'Are you all right?' he asked with an anxious frown.

She drew a little quavering breath. 'Yes, I think so.' She was beginning to wonder if she'd be able to manage on her own in the cottage after all.

'You're not to worry,' Henry told her. 'I'll find a sensible woman to look after you till you're fit again. I won't leave you till you're settled.'

She smiled tremulously. 'You're a good man, Henry, it's a comfort to know I can leave it all to you.'

They reached the station wagon and he settled her into the passenger seat. 'We'll be in Ribbenhall in twenty minutes,' he said reassuringly. 'You'll have a nice cup of tea in your own home. You'll soon begin to feel yourself again.' He got in and started the engine.

Before they reached the gates he had to halt to allow passage to an ambulance. Opposite the gates was a small shop, a newsagent and tobacconist. As they sat waiting the shopkeeper came out and set a newspaper board down on the pavement. Henry glanced across and read the words chalked in bold capitals on the board: LONGMEAD TEACHER'S BODY FOUND IN COTTAGE. He gave a sharp exclamation.

Aunt Miriam glanced up at him with anxiety. 'What is it?' she asked.

'Nothing,' he said with automatic reassurance. 'Just something I remembered. I'll pop over to the shop, I won't be a moment.' Before she could answer he opened the door and was gone.

In the shop he bought a newspaper and a carton of ice-cream. He unfolded the paper and swiftly found the little paragraph in the Stop Press. He ran his eye rapidly over it: Body of Janet Marshall, village schoolteacher, found this morning at her home, Rose Cottage, Longmead. Believed to have been dead for some time.

He drew a long trembling breath and remained staring down at the paragraph for several seconds, then he thrust the paper into his pocket and stood leaning against a display cabinet with his eyes closed. After another moment or two he drew a deep breath, shook his head and went out again into the stifling heat.

'I bought you some ice-cream,' he told Aunt Miriam. 'I know you're fond of it.' He drove out through the gates and a few minutes later they reached the Ribbenhall road.

Another ten miles to Aunt Miriam's cottage. As soon as she was settled he must slip out to the village phone and ring the Cannonbridge police.

'I was painting my fence all that Friday afternoon,' George Pickthorn said. 'I was facing Mayfield Lane the whole time.' His skin looked lined and yellow, the whites of his eyes were faintly bloodshot. 'I'm certain I'd have seen anyone walking along the lane. And heard them.' He was standing beside Chief Inspector Kelsey in the garden of Brookside. The Chief was looking at the meadow that stretched from the boundary fence up to the crossroads. George followed his gaze.

'I can't see that anyone could have crossed that meadow,' he said. It had not yet been cut. Before the police search began there had been no sign of passage through it, now it was criss-crossed with tracks, beaten-down grass.

I'm inclined to agree with him, Kelsey thought. It was of course possible for anyone wishing to cross the meadow to have skirted the edge, leaving no track through the grass, but he would still have had to get from the meadow into the lane. And to do that he would have had to negotiate a barbed-wire fence, clear a brook some five feet across and six feet deep, scramble up the bank, get through or over a tall thorn hedge—again protected by barbed wire—and then drop down into the lane. All without being seen or heard by Pickthorn painting his fence, old Mrs Perrin knitting on the porch of the first Mayfield cottage and Mrs Bryant taking her ease on the porch of the second.

'You were in your garden all afternoon?' Kelsey said.

'From a quarter past one till half past four. I saw Miss Marshall go past on her way back to school after lunch. She was a bit later than usual, she was hurrying. She didn't have time for a word, she just waved and went on.'

Kelsey slid a glance at Pickthorn. He looked fit and strong for his age. And he seemed uncommonly fond of chatting to little girls. He had gone so far as to buy a bungalow that ensured a steady trickle of little girls past his garden in term-time. Might not his tastes extend to handsome young women? Certainly Pickthorn wouldn't need to scramble across meadows or brooks, up and down banks, in and out of barbed wire in order to reach Rose

Cottage. All he would have to do was sidle up the lane and back again, with no greater hazard than sneaking past two women on porches, Mrs Bryant by her own account probably asleep most of the time, and Mrs Perrin getting on in years, probably never quite sure when she sat down in a rocking-chair whether she dozed off or not.

Pickthorn suddenly saw the quality of the look in the Chief's sharp green eyes. 'You surely don't think—' he began in tones of fierce protest.

'I don't think anything,' Kelsey said blandly. 'I'm simply trying to learn the facts.' He gazed reflectively at Pickthorn. 'Was there anyone with you that afternoon? For any part of the time?'

'No, I was working on my own, I always do.'

'Did anyone speak to you after Miss Marshall went past on her way home at a quarter past four? Someone going by, perhaps, stopping for a word?'

Pickthorn looked about with an agitated air. 'I can't think of anyone. I went inside for my tea at half past four, I always do that. I didn't come out again till twenty past five, that was a bit earlier than usual because I wanted to finish the fence. I saw the police car go past as I started painting again. I'd just about finished and cleared up when the storm broke.'

So there's only his word for where he was between half past four and twenty past five, Kelsey registered. He may have been inside the bungalow, drinking his tea, and then again he may not. The church clock struck the half-hour, jerking him out of his thoughts—time he was on his way to Cannonbridge. He'd have to leave Mayfield Farm and the two cottages for the time being.

Kelsey had just returned to the main Cannonbridge police station from the mortuary when a call was put through to his office.

'It's a Mr Henry Lloyd,' the desk sergeant said. 'The

Longmead headmaster. He's ringing from a call-box over at Ribbenhall, he's just heard about Janet Marshall.'

Over the phone Lloyd's voice sounded unsteady, distressed. The news had been a terrible shock, he could scarcely credit it.

'We have the result of the post mortem now,' Kelsey told him. Death by strangulation. With her own scarf, a slim silky affair matching her blouse, designed to be worn loosely folded over beneath the open collar. The scarf had been pulled so tightly round her neck that it had sunk deep into the flesh. But Kelsey didn't pass on these details to the headmaster. 'Quite definitely murder,' he said. 'No doubt of it.' At the other end of the phone he heard a long indrawn breath that was almost a sob.

'I'm stuck over here for a few days,' Lloyd said. 'I simply can't leave the old lady on her own, she's very far from well.'

'Don't worry,' Kelsey said. 'I understand how you're placed.'

'I'm afraid the cottage isn't on the phone, if you did want to contact me.' Lloyd broke off to insert more coins.

'There are one or two points we can clear up now,' Kelsey said when Lloyd came on again. 'Your wife picked you up as usual that Friday afternoon?' The last day anyone had seen—or had admitted to seeing—Janet Marshall alive. The medical evidence hadn't been able to pinpoint the time of death but nothing in the evidence quarrelled with the idea that she had died during the late afternoon of that day.

'That's right,' Lloyd said.

'Did you have any contact with Miss Marshall after she left the school that afternoon?'

'None at all.'

'Was there anything unusual about her behaviour that day—or during the few days immediately before? Did she seem worried or anxious, unusually quiet or preoccupied?

Did you notice anything at all out of the ordinary?'

'No, nothing, she seemed very much as usual. I was talking to her only a minute or two before she left that afternoon.' His voice broke. After a moment he said, 'It was just ordinary chat, she seemed well and cheerful.'

'Do you know of any particular friends she had? Men friends, that is?'

'I'm afraid not, but I wouldn't expect to know. I never heard of any men friends but she didn't talk much about herself, at least not to me.'

'Did she say if she was going away? Or if she was expecting any visitors?'

'I don't know about any visitors. She did mention earlier in the week that she hadn't yet decided where she was going at the end of term but she rather thought it would be to her married sister in Hadleigh.'

'One other thing,' Kelsey said. 'Were you or your wife ever inside Rose Cottage? For the fingerprints, you understand.' There were very few prints in the cottage, Janet appeared to have dusted and polished too regularly and thoroughly for that.

'No, I never had occasion to call at the cottage. I can't be absolutely sure about my wife but I don't think she ever called there. I'll be phoning her this evening, I can ask her then.'

'That's all for the moment then. You can call in at the station when you get back home,' Kelsey said without urgency. 'In the meantime, if you do think of anything that might be useful, anything at all, you can give me a ring here.'

After he had rung off Kelsey sat with his hands clasped in front of him. He had never met Lloyd but Constable Drew had met him more than once. 'A scholarly type,' the constable said. 'Always very civil. Never any trouble with discipline but the children aren't cowed, they're a bright, lively lot, alert and friendly.'

From what Drew had seen, the headmaster and Miss Marshall were on good terms. 'They behaved politely to each other,' he said, 'but not stiffly, not as if they were covering up dislike, putting a good face on it in front of an outsider.' Drew had seen more than one pantomime of that sort in the course of his visits to schools.

The Chief dismissed Lloyd from his mind. That lad Egan, he pondered, running up the road like that at ten past five. He looked down at his notes. Egan lived over in Stanbourne, lodged with a Mrs Turnbull, Prospect Place. He ran a finger along his upper lip. Janet Marshall had taught in Stanbourne for seven years before she came to Longmead. He did some swift mental arithmetic. Egan was twenty-one, according to Mrs Bryant, so he'd have left Stanbourne school ten years ago—three years before Miss Marshall began teaching there.

According to the two Mayfield girls it was they who had first spoken to Egan that Friday afternoon, not he to them. It seemed the merest chance that he had walked along the lane in the company of Janet and the girls.

He stood up. He had to get over to Hadleigh, see what Lisa Schofield had to say, he'd leave Egan for the present, the lad would probably call in at the village hall. He left his office, picked up Sergeant Lambert and swept him out to the car.

'Janet Marshall doesn't appear to have been the type to make enemies,' the Chief said when they were on their way to Hadleigh. He leaned back and closed his eyes. 'She seems to have been liked and respected, she was certainly reserved but apparently not in a way people resented.' He was beginning to build up a picture of her temperament. Self-sufficient, with plenty of interests outside her schoolwork, most of them solitary, reading, sewing, sketching, gardening, walking, listening to music.

There was no sign of any break-in at the cottage and no sign of any attempt at theft. Janet's shoulder-bag lay on the table beside the items she had brought from school and started to unpack; there were a few pounds in a purse inside the bag. In a drawer of the bureau was an unsecured cash-box containing notes and coins amounting to some eighty pounds. In the same drawer was a cheque-book and cheque guarantee card, bank and savings books, all apparently undisturbed.

'They think in the village it was some maniac,' Lambert said. 'Not a maniac from the village of course, it's never that, some outsider who spotted her on the bus or in Cannonbridge and took a violent fancy to her, found out where she lived, came knocking at the door and somehow got her to admit him, made advances to her, ended up killing her.' The post mortem hadn't been able to establish with certainty if there'd been any sexual assault; the state of the body prevented that.

'Of course it could have been a maniac,' Lambert ruminated, 'but a maniac who knew her. Not some random nutter but someone from the village. Or from Stanbourne. He could have called at Rose Cottage on a perfectly legitimate errand. She could have admitted him quite freely. And then all at once he goes berserk. I assume it is a he,' he added. 'It hardly seems a woman's crime.'

Kelsey gave a grunt. At this stage he wasn't prepared to commit himself to any view, however generalized. The first thought in most people's minds when violent crime crossed their path was that it must have been committed by a passing maniac. They seemed unable to tolerate the notion that it could have been—as in the end it usually turned out to be—the bosom friend, the lover, husband, mate at work.

Or the chap next door.

CHAPTER 10

As soon as Sergeant Lambert halted the car outside Ivydene Derek Schofield opened the front door and came down the path towards them. His colour was normal and he seemed a good deal steadier; he had dressed and shaved with care.

Kelsey told him the results of the post mortem and Schofield closed his eyes briefly. 'Lisa's upstairs,' he said after a moment. 'Lying down. I've had a terrible time with her.' His face creased into deep lines of anxiety.

'We have to talk to her,' Kelsey said. 'We'll make it as easy as we can.'

Schofield gave a nod. 'Yes, I understand. I'll go up and tell her what you've just told me. I'll give her a few minutes to calm down and then I'll bring her downstairs.'

'Take your time,' Kelsey said. 'We'll stay out here for a few minutes, we'll wander round the garden.'

Schofield went rapidly back into the house, leaving the front door propped open with an old fire-dog. Kelsey glanced about at the lawn and flowerbeds, he wandered round the side of the house and stood looking at the rear of the property. Well laid out and well cared for, fruit and vegetables, a sizable shrubbery, a solid brick wall enclosing it all. And the house—he stepped back and looked up at it—substantial, plenty of character, in good repair. 'Worth a bob or two,' he said to Lambert.

They went back to the front garden and into the house. Spacious entrance hall, good cornice work, some very agreeable watercolours. Kelsey recognized the same hand that had executed the landscapes on the walls of Rose Cottage—Robert L. Marshall, the girls' father.

From the bedroom upstairs came the low tones of

Schofield's voice, the sound of female crying on a strongly hysterical note. Kelsey drew a long resigned breath and exchanged glances with Sergeant Lambert.

They went on through an open door on the left into a long sitting-room full of soft feathery light filtering in through the trees. It was pleasantly furnished with some good old pieces. And more watercolours. Kelsey began to feel he could pick out the work of Robert L. Marshall from that of a thousand other hands.

A few minutes later Schofield came downstairs, supporting Lisa with an arm round her shoulders. She looked more like the distraught young daughter of the house than its mistress. She wore a fancy blue satin wrap and a pair of highly ornate blue satin mules trimmed with fluffy white feathers—honeymoon leftovers, Kelsey surmised. Her long blonde hair was freshly combed and she had dabbed powder over a face pink and puffy from weeping. She had paused long enough to drench herself with a French perfume that Lambert—more of a connoisseur in such matters than Kelsey, whose education had ceased at Chanel No. 5—recognized as Cabochard. He gave an appreciative little sniff.

Schofield didn't introduce Lisa, he didn't so much as glance at the two policemen as he led her to the sofa and carefully settled her among the cushions. 'I'll make some tea,' he said. He gave her a reassuring pat on the arm and went busily off to the kitchen.

Lisa lay back with her eyes closed; she seemed to be hanging on to self-control with a great effort. The Chief made no attempt to speak to her.

After a few minutes Schofield came back carrying a tray. When he had poured the tea and distributed the cups he sat down close beside his wife. She raised herself up a little and began to sip her tea, staring down at her cup.

'I imagine you've talked things over since this morning,'

Kelsey said in the most unmenacing tone of which he was capable. 'I'd be glad to hear anything either of you can tell me that might be of the slightest interest.'

Lisa suddenly began to utter little choking cries. Schofield took her cup from her and set it down. He put an arm round her shoulders and made indeterminate soothing noises.

Lisa looked across at Kelsey and the tears ran unchecked down her face. 'I thought she'd turned against me,' she said in a faltering voice, barely audible. 'And all the time—' She began to cry in an unrestrained, broken-hearted way, like a child. 'I said some horrible things about her.' She leaned against her husband's arm, shaking and crying. 'Derek wanted to take me over to see her but I wouldn't go. If we'd gone over and talked to her, if we'd arranged to pick her up that Friday afternoon—' She burst into a fresh stream of sobs. 'It's all my fault—'

'Of course it isn't,' Schofield said with force. 'How could it possibly be your fault?' He tried to quieten her, tried to persuade her to drink some tea.

In between spasmodic outbursts from Lisa, Kelsey managed a dialogue of sorts with Schofield. They'd heard nothing from Janet during the last two or three weeks of term; they'd been hoping she would come over to stay as soon as term ended.

'The arrangement was that she could come whenever it suited her,' Schofield said. 'She could let me know and I'd go over to collect her, or she could come over on the bus and I could go over later to fetch any luggage she hadn't been able to manage.'

'When was this arrangement made?' Kelsey asked.

'The last time we saw her. We went over to Rose Cottage one Sunday afternoon—' He worked it out. 'That would be July 6th. Then Lisa wrote to Janet later that week, saying she'd like her to come over as soon as she could after term ended, but she didn't get a reply.'

Prompt on cue Lisa burst into another volley of sobs. 'I'm afraid Lisa rather concluded Janet didn't want to come,' Schofield said. 'She thought she was fed up with her.'

He turned the cup in his saucer and stared down at it. 'I didn't think that was how it was at all. I thought Janet might be trying to make Lisa more independent, she might feel it would be better if she stayed away, if she gave Lisa a chance to grow up.'

Lisa went on crying loudly and hopelessly. By now they had all given up trying to stop her, they did their best to ignore the sound. 'We didn't do anything about it,' Schofield said with a note of profound apology. 'I couldn't see any point in keeping on pressing Janet if she didn't want to come. I thought she'd probably gone to stay with her friend Alison Collett in Chalford Bay, she told us Alison had asked her.'

'You didn't go over to Rose Cottage to check?' Kelsey asked with an absent-minded air.

Schofield looked surprised. 'No, we didn't see her again after we went over there for tea that Sunday.'

'Had she invited you both to tea that Sunday?' Kelsey asked with the same air of half attention.

'Well, no.' Schofield made a little apologetic movement of his head.

'So why did you go over?'

'Lisa wanted to ask her about the holiday.'

Kelsey glanced levelly at him. 'I wondered if you'd had the same thought that last Friday of term, if you decided to pop over to Rose Cottage, see if you could persuade Janet to come back with you there and then.'

'I don't follow this,' Schofield said with a frown. 'I've already told you neither Lisa nor I had any contact with Janet after that Sunday, but you take no account of that, you ask me if I went over at the end of term. Are you suggesting something?'

Kelsey maintained his steady look. 'If you'd just answer

the question: Did you go over to Rose Cottage on Friday, July 25th?'

The colour rose in Schofield's cheeks. 'I did not,' he said with fierce emphasis. There was a brief silence.

'What precisely did you do that Friday?' Kelsey asked pleasantly.

'That's the day I went over to stay with Carole Gardiner,' Lisa said suddenly in a tone that sounded almost normal. 'Carole's a friend of mine in Cannonbridge.' She glanced at her husband. 'Derek had one of his throats, he didn't go into the office, he stayed at home.'

'That's right,' Schofield said. 'Lisa phoned the firm to explain, when she got to Cannonbridge. I was here all day, in bed. I have to be careful with these throats, I'm liable to quinsy if I don't take them in time.'

He'd spent most of the day dozing; no one had called at the house. Lisa returned early on Saturday evening, he was in bed asleep when she got home.

Kelsey then asked about Janet's friends, in particular if she had any men friends.

'Not as far as we know.' Schofield glanced at Lisa for confirmation and she shook her head. 'She just didn't seem interested,' he added.

'Alison Collett was her best friend,' Lisa said, maintaining her air of greater steadiness. 'She had other friends—girl-friends—when she was at college but she didn't keep up with any of them.'

'That last Sunday when you went to tea at Rose Cottage,' Kelsey said suddenly to Schofield, 'did any kind of disagreement take place between yourself and Janet? Any quarrel?'

Schofield shook his head. 'No, nothing like that.'

'How would you describe the atmosphere between you on that occasion?'

Schofield tilted his head to one side. 'Friendly on my

side,' he said after a moment. 'Polite but rather cool on Janet's. That was her usual manner towards me,' he added.

Kelsey got to his feet. 'I'd like you both to come over to Rose Cottage some time tomorrow. To see if you think anything has been taken.' He glanced at Schofield. 'If your wife really can't face it, then come over by yourself. You can phone the station to fix a time.'

Lisa didn't come to the door with her husband when the two men left but lay back against the cushions with her eyes closed and an air of overpowering fatigue. As they walked off down the path Kelsey heard the sound of her crying drifting out behind them, thin and mewling, like that of a baby.

CHAPTER 11

Janet Marshall's solicitors were Messrs Garfitt and Hodge, a small old-fashioned firm in Cannonbridge, the firm her mother had used. On Tuesday morning Sergeant Lambert went in through the mahogany doors to keep an appointment with old Mr Garfitt, a brisk and keen-eyed seventy.

Garfitt sat behind his leather-topped desk with the tips of his fingers placed together. 'You want to know about Miss Marshall's assets and dispositions.' He glanced over some papers. 'She made a will last autumn, after her mother died. It's not a long or complicated document, her affairs were very straightforward.' There was a bequest to Mrs Alison Collett, small bequests to the two Collett children, a gift to Stanbourne church, some charitable donations. The rest went absolutely to her sister, Lisa Schofield.

'The house, Ivydene, also goes to the sister,' Garfitt

said, 'by virtue of the conditions laid down in Mrs Marshall's will. She left the house to her daughters jointly and to the survivor absolutely.'

Janet had owned a fair-sized holding of shares and a sizable sum invested in gilts and building societies. There was also an endowment policy taken out when she first began teaching. The capital sum to be paid out on the policy—to her sister—was fifteen thousand pounds. 'All in all,' Garfitt said with an inclination of his head, 'a very tidy inheritance for Mrs Schofield.'

A few minutes later Lambert walked out through the mahogany doors and made his way along the High Street to Janet's bank. He learned nothing there that was startling or even mildly surprising. She had held an account there for seven years and had maintained it with scrupulous care, she had never needed an overdraft. In recent years there had been an increasing surplus which she had regularly invested.

'She was thrifty and careful in all her financial dealings,' the manager said. 'When she had money to invest she listened to advice but she used her own judgment too, she made shrewd choices.'

Lambert's next call was at Schofield's bank in Market Street. The manager shook his head as he glanced over the records of the account.

'A pretty dismal picture,' he said. Such funds as Schofield possessed at the time of his marriage were now almost depleted. His monthly salary cheque certainly couldn't keep up with his current rate of expenditure. He had no other source of income, no investments, no property.

'He hasn't approached us for an overdraft.' The manager looked up at Lambert with a grim little jerk of his head. 'Not that he'd get one on the strength of this.'

'I'm going over to Stanbourne,' Kelsey told Sergeant

Lambert later in the morning. 'I'll see if I can get a word
with the headmistress of Stanbourne school, see if she can
give us any lead. And while I'm over there I'll chase up
young Egan.' The lad still hadn't called in at the village
hall to offer his account of his stroll along the lane with
Miss Marshall.

Not that Kelsey was altogether surprised at this. By all
accounts Clive Egan was a shy, retiring youth who would
probably imagine there was nothing to be learned from
the few minutes he'd spent in Janet's company.

It was close to noon as the Chief walked up the path
that led to the front door of the Stanbourne schoolhouse.
Fleecy white blankets swung on a clothes-line; the lawn
was velvet-smooth, the flower borders trimly kept. The
front door stood open and the sweet ripe smell of newly-
made plum jam drifted out.

He knocked at the door and a cheerful vigorous voice
invited him to come in. He stepped inside and declared
himself.

The headmistress, Mrs Dunbar, was on her knees in the
kitchen, in front of an electric cooker. She wore stout
rubber gloves and was busy cleaning the interior of the
oven. Jars of ruby-red jam stood ranged on a thick layer of
newspapers on the table.

'You don't mind if I carry on with this?' Mrs Dunbar
said. She was a big-boned woman in late middle age with
a direct manner and a good-natured smile. Her face was
deeply flushed from her exertions.

'I'm going out to lunch at half past twelve,' she
explained. 'If I don't finish cleaning this oven now, I'll
never be able to persuade myself to tackle it again later.
It's the job above all others that I most sincerely detest.'

She conducted the conversation between bouts of fierce
scouring. 'I liked Janet,' she told the Chief. 'She was
conscientious, well-mannered, an excellent teacher. I was
very sorry when she left Stanbourne.' She gave him a swift

upward glance. 'Have you met the sister—Lisa Schofield? She was the reason for Janet leaving Stanbourne. She got married—very much against Janet's wishes.' She pursed her lips. 'And she announced her intention of bringing the bridegroom back to Ivydene to live. She had every right to do that of course, it was her house just as much as Janet's.'

'So Miss Marshall decided to clear out and leave them to it?' Kelsey said.

'She certainly had no intention of making a cosy threesome in Ivydene.' She scrubbed vigorously at the floor of the oven.

'Did she disapprove of Derek Schofield?'

She pulled a face. 'He was scarcely what she'd have chosen for her sister—he was too old for her, for one thing—but I don't know that she had anything specific against him. She didn't go into it all with me in detail, that wasn't her way. But I do know she thought he wasn't very frank and open, she felt there was something secretive about him. She didn't like that.' She gave the Chief a shrewd look. 'She wasn't a bad judge of character. And after all he was well over thirty when he met Lisa, he could have had something to hide in all that time.'

'Did Janet try to find out?' Kelsey asked. 'Did she make enquiries?'

'If she did she didn't tell me. But it wouldn't surprise me if she did, she always liked to know the facts, her feet were always very firmly on the ground.'

She sat back on her heels. 'I don't believe it ever entered Lisa's head that Janet would pack her bags and leave Ivydene. I'm sure she fancied she'd got herself a housekeeper, cook, and I don't know what else, all thrown in for free, she thought she'd be able to swan around and enjoy herself, play the mistress of the establishment, the pretty little bride, with Janet running the place and doing all the chores.'

No, she knew of no man friend of Miss Marshall's, no particular friend of either sex in Stanbourne. 'She was as friendly with me as she was with anyone,' she said. 'And that's not saying a lot. She'd have a chat over a cup of tea at morning break, but she wasn't one to go offering or accepting invitations. She wasn't offensive about it, she just made it clear that was the way she wanted it.' She looked reflective. 'I knew her mother, Mrs Marshall, she was a more outgoing type, she joined in more in village life. I sometimes went over to supper at Ivydene when she was alive.'

'Wouldn't you expect a girl with Janet's looks to have any number of men friends?' Kelsey said.

'I must admit it did surprise me at first that she didn't have any, but then I got used to it. She just didn't seem interested in men. She always had a dozen things she was doing, she was never short of an occupation. In these small villages, of course, there aren't many spare men and I imagine she'd have been pretty choosy. She never seemed aware of her looks, she wasn't in the least vain. She didn't bother with make-up or jewellery though she was always nicely dressed and well groomed. She made a lot of her own clothes—and very competently too.'

She picked up an old knife and chipped at a stubborn bit of baked-on grease. 'Certainly men noticed her. But they soon got the message.' She glanced up at the Chief. 'Is that what you think? Some man made a pass at her? She resisted and he killed her?'

The Chief raised his shoulders. 'It's only one of half a dozen possibilities.' He wasn't at all clear what the other possibilities might be. Certainly robbery didn't seem to be one of them. Derek Schofield had gone over the cottage with a constable, he didn't think anything was missing.

The Chief stood biting his lower lip. 'A lad called Egan,' he said. 'Clive Egan. He was a pupil—'

'Yes, I know Clive.' She put her head on one side and

stared critically at the results of her labours. 'That'll have
to do.' She sighed deeply and got to her feet with an
effort. 'If ever I come into a fortune,' she said with
feeling, 'the first thing I'll go out and buy will be a self-
cleaning oven.' She peeled off her rubber gloves and stood
rubbing the small of her back. 'Not a bad lad, Clive. He
had a rotten childhood.' She gave the Chief a level look. 'I
hope he's not in any trouble.'

'He's not, as far as I know.'

'I'm glad to hear it. I knew the family—the mother in
particular. She used to do a bit of work at the school,
cleaning, helping with the dinners. And she sometimes
did a bit of cleaning here for me. She was a nice woman,
cheerful, a good manager. She died when Clive was nine.'
She sighed and shook her head, staring in silence at the
jars of jam. 'It was a great blow to Clive. He began to
develop fears.'

'Would you call him a phobic type?' Kelsey asked.

She pursed her lips. 'I'm not very fond of labelling
people, I've never seen much good come of it. It seems
natural enough to me for a child to grow a little fearful of
the world after his mother has been suddenly snatched
away out of it. How can he tell what will happen next?
How can he trust anything in life to stay the same, to be
what it appears to be? I think it would be a much more
abnormal reaction to respond to a deeply distressing
situation as if it was perfectly ordinary, no cause for
concern.'

'What form did these fears take?'

'Nothing very spectacular. He wouldn't sit at the front
of the class any more, he had to sit with his back against a
wall. And he couldn't stand up and speak in front of the
class, that sort of thing, it's not uncommon when children
are disturbed.' She flicked a glance at Kelsey. 'And there
were difficulties with his father.'

'What sort of difficulties?'

'He started drowning his sorrows at the Greyhound after his wife died. I had a pretty shrewd notion he was knocking Clive about, he started flinching at a sudden movement—that's often a give-away.' A wasp flew in at the window and buzzed round the jam. She snatched up a dishcloth and dealt it a shrewd swipe.

'Did you do anything about it?' Kelsey asked.

She picked up the wasp and flung it out into the blue summer air. 'I did try to speak to the father but he wouldn't make any kind of response, he seemed overcome with shame—but things didn't improve. I asked the Vicar to speak to him, he tried but he didn't have any better success. Then I tried talking to Clive—that isn't always the wisest thing to do but I couldn't think of anything else. But Clive wouldn't open up, he just stayed mute and stubborn, he'd got to be like that after his mother died, he was never like that before, he was always a very nice-natured little boy.' She blew out a little mournful breath.

'In the end I took a chance and asked him a couple of direct questions but he denied there was anything wrong.' She raised her shoulders. 'So I left it at that. A year or so later Clive left Stanbourne school and went to the Comprehensive in Cannonbridge, so he wasn't on my conscience any more.' She gave the Chief a direct look. 'It isn't always easy in that kind of situation, there isn't any obvious course of action. You can do as much harm by interfering as by doing nothing.'

She shook her head. 'In the end the father was killed, knocked down by a car one night when he was drunk. A solution of sorts, I suppose. But of course by that time Clive was eighteen or so. His childhood, whatever it had been, good or ill, was over, it was what it was, it couldn't be made over into something else.'

She stared out of the window. 'He was always fond of reading, I think that helped him more than anything. It's never so bad when a child has something—anything—to hang on to. He always had his head in a book, he read every book in our little school library. I've often known him walk along the road reading—' She broke off suddenly.

'You've remembered something,' Kelsey said.

She frowned. 'No, nothing really.'

'I'd like to know what it was,' Kelsey said. 'I won't jump to conclusions.'

'It was just—' She hesitated. 'I don't suppose it means anything, it just came into my mind. A young teacher we had here at that time, a young married woman, she taught the Infants—when Clive was in the juniors, he was never in her class. After his mother died, some little time afterwards, a couple of months perhaps, he took to hanging round the school at the end of the afternoon, going into the Infants' classroom where this teacher would be clearing up or preparing work. He'd ask her if there were any jobs he could do, any errands to run. Then he started hanging round her house in the evenings and at weekends. She'd look out of the window and there he'd be, standing by the gate.'

'Nothing more than that? He didn't do anything?'

She shook her head. 'No, he never did anything. He wasn't actually a nuisance but it worried her, she spoke to me about it. We didn't want to be hard on him, we knew how he was grieving over his mother. Anyway, not long afterwards her husband got promotion and they moved away from this area, down to Bristol, so that was the end of it.'

'And the teacher that replaced her? Did he start hanging round her?'

'No, it simply stopped. Then before much longer he went off to the Cannonbridge school.'

'The teacher he hung around,' Kelsey said. 'What did she look like?'

She gave him a long, thoughtful look. 'She was a

pleasant-looking young woman, nothing special, you wouldn't glance twice at her in the street. Medium build, straight fair hair, spectacles.' She tilted her head back. 'Clive's in digs now with a Mrs Turnbull, she's a widow, getting on a bit, a sensible, homely sort of woman. It seems to work very well.'

'Do you know if Clive's working round here today?'

'Yes, he's doing some repairs at the old smithy, it's been done up as a cottage. I saw him there yesterday, he told me the job would last another couple of days.'

She gave the Chief directions as she rinsed her rubber gloves and hung them up to dry.

As Kelsey drove up to the old smithy he could see a high platform constructed of planks and trestles set against the side wall, with a ladder leading up to it. A tall, strongly-built young man was kneeling on the platform with his back to the Chief, pointing the stonework. He glanced down as Kelsey halted his car. The Chief got out and stood looking up at him.

'Clive Egan?' he called up and the young man gave a nod. 'Police. I'd like a word with you.'

Clive set down his trowel and upended his handhawk on a pile of mortar. He came down the ladder without haste and stood in silence waiting for the Chief to open his mouth. Across the fields came the droning beat of a combine harvester, the warm scents of summer.

Kelsey glanced at the house. 'There's no one at home,' Clive said. 'They're both out at work all day in Cannonbridge.'

Kelsey gave him a long, assessing look. Not a bad-looking lad, an air at once unforthcoming and mildly aggressive, like a woodland animal. Eyes like a fox, the colour of a golden topaz, quick and sharp, full of light.

'I dare say you've read the papers,' Kelsey said, 'You know what's happened over at Longmead.' Clive gave another brief nod. 'I fancied you'd have called in at the village hall before this,' Kelsey added.

A look of surprise crossed the lad's face. 'Me? Why would you expect me to go over there?'

'To tell us about your dealings with Miss Marshall.'

'I didn't have any dealings with her,' Clive said on an astonished note.

'You walked along the lane with her on the last day of term.'

'Only in a manner of speaking. I was walking along with Jill Bryant, I know the Bryants. Miss Marshall and Heather Abell, they just happened to be walking along too.'

'But you did talk to Miss Marshall?'

'Well, yes, but it was just ordinary chat, making conversation. She asked me about my job, that sort of thing.'

Kelsey eyed him reflectively. 'So you walked along, chatting. And then what? Come on, lad, speak up, I want to know exactly what happened. Every little detail that day is of interest to us.'

Clive gestured with mild exasperation. 'Nothing happened. She walked on to her cottage. I stayed talking to the girls for a few minutes, then I walked off up the lane. I didn't see Miss Marshall again, I never gave her another thought.'

'A handsome young woman,' Kelsey said. 'You never gave her another thought.'

The colour rose in Clive's cheeks. He made no reply but stood with his arms close into his sides, his fists tightly clenched. With his athletic build and close-clipped fair hair he looked like a recalcitrant German soldier in an old war film.

'That was around half past four,' Kelsey said. 'Your bus didn't arrive till just before five-fifteen. You had to run to catch it. It didn't take you three-quarters of an hour to walk up the lane. What were you doing in that time?'

'I was reading,' Clive said at once. 'I sat down on the bank at the side of the lane, there's an old tree-trunk there, it makes a good seat.' Kelsey had noticed the bole of the tree, a comfortable little spot, a few yards further on up the lane from Rose Cottage. 'I always have a book with me,' Clive added.

'And while you were sitting there reading, did you see anyone go past, up or down the lane?'

'No.'

'Or across the meadow?' Again Clive shook his head.

'You might have been so wrapped up in your book—'

'I'd have noticed,' Clive said with certainty. 'I couldn't fail to, the lane's very narrow.'

'Did you hear any sounds from Rose Cottage? Any cries or voices? Did you see anyone go in at the gate? Or anywhere near the cottage? In the garden perhaps?'

'No.' He shook his head with resolution. 'But I wouldn't be able to see the gate from where I was sitting, the lane curves round. And the cottage stands back from the road. I wouldn't expect to be able to hear anything either.'

'You're sure you were reading all that time? You didn't follow Miss Marshall up to the cottage and get yourself asked in for a drink of squash—on such a hot day?'

The golden eyes jerked wide open, full of angry light. 'No, I did not. I never went near the cottage.'

Kelsey suddenly produced a plastic bag from his pocket and held it out, turning it over so that Clive could see both sides of what it held—a used envelope that had been folded vertically into four and was now straightened out again. The envelope was addressed to Mrs Turnbull at Prospect Place and on the reverse was written in a careful elderly hand: 25 lbs or a bit over. Wanted for dinner Aug. 2nd. Can they deliver?

'Ever seen that before?' Kelsey said.

'Yes, it's the note Mrs Turnbull gave me, it's the order

for her turkey.' Clive explained about the golden wedding dinner, how he'd walked up to Mayfield during his dinner-hour that Friday to deliver the message.

'What did you do with the envelope after you left the farm?' Kelsey asked.

'I folded it and used it as a bookmark,' Clive said.
'Where did you find it?'

Kelsey didn't answer. It had been found during the minute search of the area, in the bole of the dead tree at the side of the lane, near Rose Cottage, in among dead leaves and old grass. The envelope was dry, the ink unsmudged by rain.

'Did you use it as a bookmark before you went to the farm that day?' Kelsey said. 'When you were eating your dinner?'

Clive shook his head. 'No, I wouldn't do that, not before I'd delivered the message.'

'And after you left the farm, when you got back to the house where you were working, did you sit down and start reading then?'

'No, there wasn't time, I started working right away.'

Kelsey stared at him for a few moments longer and Clive held himself rigid under the scrutiny. 'You'd better call in at the hall,' the Chief said abruptly. 'Make a statement. Get your prints taken.' The lad's head jerked up at that. 'Matter of routine,' Kelsey added. 'Doesn't imply anything.' He made a dismissive gesture, turned away and got back into his car. By the time he had started the engine and moved off, Clive was once more up on his platform, hard at work again on the pointing.

CHAPTER 12

Kelsey sat at his desk looking down at his notes. It's a period of just under an hour that most directly concerns us, he thought. Janet Marshall left the two girls and walked on to her cottage at, say, four-eighteen. At five-fourteen or so the girls knocked at her door and got no reply. It very much looked as if it was between those two points that she was attacked, if not finally killed.

He twirled a pencil between his fingers. No doubt who benefited by the death—the Schofields.

Assuming that Lisa was where she said she was that Friday afternoon, with her friend Carole Gardiner out at Leabarrow, what about Derek Schofield? There was only his word that he'd stayed huddled in bed or slopping about the house all day in his dressing-gown. He could easily have nipped out and driven over to Longmead, could have left his car by the old quarry, well back out of sight under thick overhanging trees. He would have had to arrive at a time when Janet was at the cottage to let him in—there was no sign of any forced entry and it was highly unlikely that either Schofield or Lisa would have a key to the property.

He frowned fiercely and scratched his forehead with the pencil. The only prints of Schofield's in the cottage were a couple on the back of a chest of drawers in the bedroom, there were none of Lisa's. Schofield told them he'd helped Janet move the chest the second or third time he and Lisa had visited the cottage.

Right—so Janet has to be at home for Schofield to be able to get into the cottage, and Janet didn't get home that day till, say, four-twenty. The problem was: how could Schofield have approached the property around

that time without being seen? If he'd darted across the
field to the back of the cottage he'd have been seen by the
two Mayfield farmworkers busy on the fencing. Suppose
instead he'd walked boldly along Quarry Lane, along the
Hayford road, past the school, and up Mayfield Lane?
George Pickthorn was in his garden painting his fence
until four-thirty and the two women at Mayfield Cottages
were on their porches till after five.

Kelsey rattled the pencil against his teeth. That way
was just possible — if Schofield got to Mayfield Lane after
four-thirty, when Pickthorn had gone in for his tea, and
the two women chanced to be dozing as he sneaked past.
But surely that was all far too much of a gamble — no,
Schofield would never have taken such a chance.

Ah — what if he'd gone over to Longmead much
earlier, say during the dinner-hour, timing his call at the
cottage for about one o'clock? Kelsey sat up with a feeling
of exhilaration; that was more like it. Janet would be
there to admit him, she'd have just about finished her
lunch. And there'd be no one around to see him arrive,
whichever of the two routes he'd chosen from Quarry
Lane. Ken Bryant, Neil Fleming and George Pickthorn,
all indoors, eating; the schoolchildren not yet out in the
playground, still bending their heads over helpings of
pudding; the two women at Mayfield Cottages indoors,
busy with pans and dishes. In all probability Schofield
would run across the field to the back of the cottage, the
Chief decided; in his shoes that's certainly what I would
have done.

He put up a hand and cupped his mouth, pressing the
fingers into his cheeks. So — Schofield reaches the back
door and knocks, Janet lets him in. He talks to her, he
says: Are you coming over to Ivydene soon? He chats
about Lisa and so on. He tells her about his money
difficulties, points out Lisa's extravagant ways, the fact
that she won't get her legacy from her mother for another

seven years, that she got nothing under her father's will. Could Janet possibly help them out, lend them some money, even perhaps make over her half of Ivydene to Lisa—but at the back of his mind is the half-thought, not fully formulated: If she refuses, if she's adamant, I may be compelled to take steps. It's because of that shadowy thought that he's taken care not to be seen or heard approaching the cottage, not to mention to anyone, Lisa included, that he intends going over there.

Janet refuses his request, she says they must sort things out for themselves. He makes light of her refusal, he says: Oh well, no harm in asking, something's bound to turn up.

Janet says: I must go, I'll be late back to school. He says: You don't mind if I stay on here for a few minutes to make myself a cup of coffee? I'll lock up properly when I go. She says, Yes, all right. Why wouldn't she? She goes off in a rush.

Schofield passes the next three hours as best he may. He makes his coffee, takes his time over it, clears up, dozes, broods, waits for her to return.

When at last he hears her open the garden gate he unlatches the door leading to the stairs, steps inside and closes the door behind him.

Janet comes into the cottage, sets down her things and begins to unpack them, she pours herself a drink of squash. She hears a noise from the stairs. She turns—and there he is.

Later he wipes away any fingerprints, checks he's left no incriminating evidence, sits down and waits for darkness to fall.

There's a knock at the front door. He freezes, then he hears the voices of children and he breathes again. They go round to the back door and knock again. He lies doggo.

The children go off, no one else calls. He's not worried

on that score; he knows Janet doesn't have many callers and, however many they are, they're not likely to break down the door to get in when she doesn't answer.

It grows dark much earlier than usual, it's brewing up for a storm. By seven-fifteen the rain is drumming down. No one in the fields, no one on porches, in gardens. He puts his jacket over his head, lets himself out, runs across the field to the quarry parking place, jumps into his car and drives off.

When he gets home it's straight back into pyjamas and dressing-gown, back into bed. But he needn't worry, he isn't expecting callers, and there's no house close enough to observe his comings and goings. Ivydene isn't on the phone so he doesn't even have to worry that Lisa—or anyone else—might have phoned while he was out, might remember later that there was no answer.

Kelsey threw down his pencil. I'll have another word with Lisa, he decided. She'd had time now to calm down and a word while her husband was out might produce interesting revelations.

He looked at his watch. A bit late to go calling at Ivydene today, Schofield would soon be getting in from work. Better leave it till tomorrow morning, go along, say, at about ten, give her time to get out of bed. He had a shrewd notion Madame Lisa wasn't the type to rise at dawn to scrub the kitchen floor.

Shortly before ten next morning Sergeant Lambert drove Kelsey out to Hadleigh.

Lisa seemed a good deal steadier when she answered their ring at the door, although her face was still a little blurred and puffy. Her long blonde hair was twisted up into a loose knot on top of her head. She looked very young and very pretty.

She led the way into the sitting-room and arranged herself to advantage on the sofa; she seemed to have assumed the role of invalid, whether because of her pregnancy, her bereavement or a combination of the two, the Chief couldn't guess. She asked no questions but sat waiting for him to speak.

'I was wondering if you'd been in touch with Mrs Collett, Alison Collett,' he said. 'I wondered if you'd contacted her of if she'd heard about what's happened from some other source and contacted you.'

Lisa shook her head. 'No, we haven't been in touch with her. Derek and I talked about it last night and we decided we'd write her a letter this evening.' She lit a cigarette and inhaled deeply. I'll go over to Chalford Bay on Saturday, Kelsey thought, see if the Colletts can throw any light.

He led Lisa on to talk about her life at Ivydene, her marriage, the old days at Ellenborough. Her manner became more relaxed, she began to smile a little as she talked. She made mention several times of "my friend Carole Gardiner" and a picture of that lady began to build up in Kelsey's mind. Easy-going, free-handed, lively.

'Your husband doesn't go over to Leabarrow with you?' he asked.

She shook her head. 'No. Carole likes going to discos. And there are some good clubs in Cannonbridge, they have top groups playing there. Derek isn't keen on that kind of thing but he doesn't mind me going.' A very convenient arrangement for Schofield, Kelsey thought, stops Madame Lisa growing sulky with boredom and no need for Derek to put his hand in his pocket and pay for these merry outings—or endure the screeches and howls of the young at play.

'Anything I want to do is all right with Derek,' Lisa said with an air of complacency. 'He'd do anything for me.' I wonder if he'd draw the line at murder, Kelsey thought. And he wondered also what she'd reply if he put that question to her.

He gazed at her contemplatively. So far this morning she hadn't so much as uttered Janet's name. He had a shrewd idea that her calm of manner was directly linked to this point, that if he were to mention the dead girl, hysterical tears would very shortly flow again.

'That day you were over at Carole Gardiner's, when your husband had one of his throats,' he began, delicately skirting the danger zone.

Lisa's hand remained arrested in the act of raising her cigarette to her lips. She flashed him a wary look.

'You didn't mind going off and leaving him alone for the night? It didn't spoil your evening—worrying about him?'

She smiled, with relief in her look. 'No, I knew there was no need to worry. He often gets these throats, he told me right at the beginning they weren't serious, not if he takes them in time. And anyway he phoned me at Carole's to say he was feeling a lot better, I wasn't to worry about him, I must go out and enjoy myself.'

Phoned her? Kelsey thought. Where had he phoned from? There was no phone at Ivydene. And no phone at Rose Cottage. If Schofield was indeed holed up in Rose Cottage waiting for the sky to darken so he could make his escape, then he couldn't at the same time be out somewhere phoning Lisa.

'What time would that be?' he asked her. 'When he phoned you?'

She wrinkled her brow. 'It was about six o'clock. Carole went out to get the evening paper so we could see what was on. He phoned while she was out—I suppose it was between a quarter past and half past six.'

Kelsey experienced a keen sense of disappointment. He could see no way in which Schofield could have got away from the cottage by that time. The two men from Mayfield Farm were working in the field at the back of the cottage until six-thirty, Schofield couldn't possibly have darted past them unseen. And if he had left by the front door and gone down Mayfield Lane, he would have been seen by George Pickthorn out painting his fence again after tea. No, if Schofield had phoned Lisa around six, then he couldn't have been in the cottage at the relevant time, he couldn't have been the killer. He exchanged a look with Sergeant Lambert—so much for Schofield as a suspect.

And then the Chief's expression changed. Hang on, he thought, Schofield could have turned the other way out of the front gate of Rose Cottage. The crossroads were clear by five-twenty, the police car gone on its way; there would have been no one round to see him if he left the cottage at, say, five-thirty, went up to the crossroads, round past the farm, then down Quarry Lane to his car. And he'd have had plenty of time to phone Lisa between six and six-thirty, he could have stopped at any one of half a dozen places on the way home; in fact that would probably be his first thought, to phone Lisa at Carole's, establish some sort of alibi, however insubstantial.

'Where did your husband phone from?' he asked with an idle air.

'From the shop,' Lisa said at once. 'The store just along the road. He popped out to get some ice-cream for his throat, he slipped a jacket and trousers on over his pyjamas.'

'He didn't mention that to us,' Kelsey said in the same casual tone. 'He told us he was here all day.'

'Well, he was,' she said with positive assurance. 'More or less. He wouldn't be away ten minutes. He wouldn't think of mentioning a little thing like that.'

Can she possibly be so naive? Kelsey wondered. He observed a look of massive scepticism on Sergeant Lambert's face. We've no word from the burning bush, the look said, to guarantee that at all times and in all places Madame Schofield speaks nothing but the unvarnished truth.

Kelsey pushed back his chair. Two visits seemed indicated, the corner shop and Carole Gardiner.

Lisa looked almost disappointed when they stood up to leave. 'It's so quiet here,' she complained. 'So deadly dull. I keep asking Derek to move to Cannonbridge and buy a nice modern bungalow but of course we can't sell this house—'

She broke off and tears rose in her eyes.

Yes, you can sell it now, Kelsey thought, you can have your dream bungalow and a substantial sum of money into the bargain.

With the aid of quick footwork and a few swift words of farewell they managed to get clear of the house before the cascade of tears actually fell.

The corner shop was situated some forty yards from Ivydene. Kelsey told Sergeant Lambert to drive on a little before he parked. He decided to despatch the sergeant inside on his own as being less likely to arouse speculation. 'Keep it all very casual,' Kelsey warned him.

Not much hope of that, Lambert thought as he walked back to the shop. A savage murder, a detective asking questions about the movements of the victim's brother-in-law, no way he could avoid rousing speculation. He reached the premises and went in.

Half a dozen youngsters crowded the interior; they were dressed in jeans and T-shirts and carried packs on their shoulders. They argued noisily over purchases of crisps and Cokes, sweets and chocolates. Lambert had a word with the woman while her husband did his best to deal with the youngsters.

Lambert kept his manner as light as possible. The woman was anxious to be helpful but no, she couldn't really cast her mind that far back. Oh yes—now the sergeant mentioned it — that was the day the schools finished, yes, she could recall that, she had children of her own. As to Mr Schofield coming in that day to use the phone, it was difficult to remember precisely, Mr or Mrs Schofield often came in to make a call.

Perhaps she could recall Mr Schofield buying ice-cream on an occasion when he also used the phone? Or looking unwell, speaking as if he had a bad throat, even making mention of a sore throat? The time could have been around six in the evening.

'I'm afraid I'm always busy at that time,' she said apologetically. 'Running in and out of the kitchen, trying to get a bit of supper going, as well as serving in here. I wouldn't be taking all that much notice.'

Perhaps it was her husband who had dealt with Mr Schofield? Yes, that was possible. She took over the serving of the unruly youngsters while Lambert put his questions to her husband.

At the mention of the sore throat the shopkeeper said, 'Oh yes, Mr Schofield's bought throat pastilles here more than once.' He gestured at a box on the shelf behind him. 'He buys those, they're what I use myself, they're very good.' No, he couldn't say when Schofield had last bought them, nor could he recall an occasion when he had bought pastilles and ice-cream together. As to phone calls, it was usually Mrs Schofield who came in to make calls, he couldn't remember Mr Schofield making more than one or two since he'd come to live at Ivydene, he certainly couldn't remember him making a call in recent weeks.

As Lambert went out and turned to close the door he saw the shopkeeper and his wife talking together in animated whispers, glancing after him, while at the other side of the counter the youngsters pushed and shoved each other unrebuked.

Kelsey wasn't surprised at Lambert's lack of success. 'A

bit much to expect them to remember clearly after that length of time,' he said. 'We'll go straight on to Leabarrow and see what Carole Gardiner has to say.'

Kelsey didn't speak during the drive to Cannonbridge but sat brooding over his talk with Lisa Schofield. Lambert drove in silence, knowing from the Chief's hunched shoulders and the frown on his freckled face that he wouldn't welcome conversation.

As they halted at the first set of traffic lights Kelsey suddenly gave a grunt; a thought had just struck him. It was clear to him — with the benefit of hindsight — that Schofield could have got from the gate of Rose Cottage to his car in Quarry Lane without being observed — but Schofield wasn't to know that at the time. It would have been taking a terrible chance. How could he be sure there wouldn't be some chance stroller in Mayfield Lane, someone working in the top field, a pair of eyes looking out of a window in the farmhouse, someone walking along Quarry Lane? Was it conceivable he would have taken such a chance?

No, Kelsey was forced to conclude as he stared moodily out at the morning shoppers, I don't think it is conceivable.

CHAPTER 13

The Leabarrow estate lay on the southern tip of Cannonbridge, on the edge of open country with magnificent long views of wooded hills. The estate was attractively landscaped with some fine mature trees left standing.

As they approached the road where the Gardiners lived, Kelsey glanced out of the car window. The houses were the kind estate agents like to call executive

detached, although the function of the word executive in
this context Kelsey had never been able precisely to
determine. And their detachment was so minimal that
not even the most resolute and emaciated householder
would be able to squeeze between them.

'Twenty years ago,' the Chief observed to Sergeant
Lambert as they parked the car under the shade of a
lordly oak, 'you could have bought a fair-sized sporting
estate—with a noble house thrown in for good
measure—for what they ask nowadays for one of these
chicken coops.'

The dwellings were box-like in construction and had a
number of pseudo-classical features stuck on in an
arbitrary and unconvincing fashion. The Gardiners'
gateposts were topped by a brace of costive-looking lions
in imitation stone and the neighbouring entrance boasted
a pair of ill-tempered owls.

The two men walked up the narrow path between trim
borders bright with dahlias and asters. The hedges had
been recently clipped, the little lawn was neatly kept,
punctuated with yellow standard roses. In the tiny porch
a piece of varnished timber, eccentrically shaped and
suspended from gilded chains, bore the name 'Cloverdale'
in extravagantly curly letters. The front windows were
ornamented with panes of fake bullseye glass.

Childish shouts and laughter echoed from the rear
garden as the Chief put a finger firmly on the bell. A
few moments later Carole Gardiner answered his ring
with a cheerful, friendly look. She was a plump, bouncy
young woman with lively green eyes and wavy chestnut
hair hanging to her shoulders in a 'forties filmstar
style.

As soon as she took in the presence on her doorstep of
two large broad-shouldered men, her face underwent a
dramatic change. Her colour drained away and she
looked as if she was about to faint. She put a hand up to

her head and leaned forward, steadying herself against the door-jamb.

Kelsey stepped over the threshold and put an arm round her shoulders; she offered no resistance. 'You must sit down,' he said with authority. On the left of the narrow hall a door stood open and he steered her towards it.

The room was brightly and expensively furnished with chainstore taste. It was scattered with children's books and toys and smelled of alcohol and tobacco. Kelsey settled her on the big squashy sofa with her feet up and her head resting against the velvet cushions.

'It's all right,' he assured her. 'We haven't brought bad news.'

She looked tremulously up at him. 'Mike—I thought—'

'Don't upset yourself,' he said soothingly. 'There's been no accident.'

She gave a long, quavering sigh and the colour began to return to her cheeks. 'My husband,' she said, 'he's on a rig. I thought for sure you'd come to tell me—' She closed her eyes and drew a deep, trembling breath.

'It's nothing to do with your husband,' Kelsey told her. 'As far as we know he's as right as rain.'

She began to smile, to laugh. 'Oh dear, what a carry-on!' she said as she swung her shapely legs to the floor. 'I'll go and make some coffee. I'm sure you'd both like a cup, and I know I would.' Her shining filmstar hair danced about her shoulders.

'You stay where you are,' Kelsey said firmly. 'Let Sergeant Lambert make the coffee. You've just had a nasty shock, it makes no difference that it wasn't justified. You needn't worry about the sergeant, he's a dab hand at coffee and he won't break a thing.'

'Oh all right,' she said, laughing. 'The kitchen's straight on down the hall.' She seemed suddenly full of joy and happiness. 'It's at the back of your mind all the time,' she said to Kelsey. 'You're always expecting bad news, you can't help it.' Her pleasure was so great that he was able to disclose the nature of his visit without at once causing speculation to run across her face.

'What a dreadful business about that poor girl,' she said. 'It gives me the creeps thinking about it. I never met her but Lisa talked about her. First thing I knew about it was I read it in the evening paper. I couldn't believe it. I said to the girl in the shop — I'd just bought a paper, I was standing there in the shop looking at it — I said: Good God, I know that woman.'

Sergeant Lambert came in with a tray holding beakers of coffee and a bowl of sugar. 'Be a dear,' Mrs Gardiner said. 'Fetch some biscuits or cakes, anything you like. There's tons of stuff back there, have a ferret round.'

Lambert hastened back to the microscopic kitchen. He'd already come across packets of biscuits and shop-bought cakes in his search for the coffee, he'd helped himself to surreptitious fig Newtons. Now he heaped a tray with legitimate plunder and carried it back to the sitting-room.

'Yes, I do remember,' Mrs Gardiner was saying. 'Lisa was here that Friday, that's the last time she came over, she stayed the night. And you think that's when it could have happened!' No, she hadn't expected Lisa to come over again since then, she never came when Mike was home, that was understood between them. He'd only been gone back to the rig a couple of days. Kelsey saw that her mind was still on her husband, she was only half attending to his questions and their possible implications.

'Help yourselves,' she urged, waving a hand at the laden tray. 'Don't wait to be asked.' She fell upon a packet of fancy iced cakes and began to eat with gusto. 'I don't know why, but I'm absolutely famished,' she said between bites. 'It must be the relief.' Against his better judgment Kelsey took a vast flaky pastry oozing with jam and cream; it looked delicious and breakfast was a long time back.

No, she couldn't say about any phone call that Friday evening. Yes, she did usually pop out for an evening paper when Lisa was here, to see if there was anything special on. And yes, Derek Schofield had rung Lisa here once or twice. But as to whether he'd rung that particular day—she was sorry but she just couldn't recall. No, Lisa hadn't been in touch with her since the discovery of her sister's body.

'I've been wondering what to do about that,' she said. 'I did think of writing her a letter but I couldn't for the life of me think what to put.'

She was now well into her second cake. 'Lisa's a good kid,' she said. 'We have a lot of laughs, stops me going mad with boredom when Mike's away.' She pulled a face. 'They're a stuck-up lot round here.' She saw Lambert eyeing a Chelsea bun with an irresolute eye. 'Go on,' she pressed him. 'You have it. You only live once.' Her face grew suddenly sober. 'That poor Janet Marshall, I woke up last night thinking about her.'

Kelsey drank his coffee. 'Derek Schofield doesn't come over here with Lisa?' he asked.

'No, thank goodness.' She reached for a pastry and began to eat it with unabated appetite.

'You don't like him?'

'I hardly know him. I'm not mad about what I do know.' She wiped a flake of pastry from the corner of her mouth. 'He seems to suit Lisa well enough.' She gave the Chief a shrewd look. 'For now, that is. I wouldn't like to bet good money she'll still be feeling the same way about him in five years' time.'

As they were driving back to the station Lambert said, 'I keep coming back to that lad, Clive Egan. Running up the lane like that—'

'He got absorbed in his book,' Kelsey said, his mind still half on Carole Gardiner. 'He lost track of the time, suddenly remembered the bus, had to sprint for it.'

'We've only his word for that,' Lambert said. 'It's never seemed a very plausible explanation to me.'

'I believe he did sit down by the side of the lane to read his book,' Kelsey said. 'That hardly suggests the time or the inclination to go murdering Janet Marshall. I can't quite see the lad strangling her and then calmly sitting down to read another chapter.'

'It could have been the other way round,' Lambert persisted. 'He sat down to read, then something happened, he heard or saw something that took him to the cottage. Or he lost interest in his book and started to think about the conversation he'd just had with Janet, he stood up and walked along to the cottage. He says something—anything—to get himself asked inside: Could she advise him about his reading? Or evening classes? He tells her he has some time before his bus goes, he'd be grateful if she could spare him a quarter of an hour. Or he may never have sat down by the tree to read at all, he could have simply left the girls, walked up the lane and turned straight in at the gate of Rose Cottage.'

'The envelope was there, inside the tree,' Kelsey pointed out.

'He could have put it there afterwards,' Lambert said stubbornly. 'He gets home and thinks: Christ, I'm in one hell of a mess. As soon as they find the body someone will remember me walking along the lane with her. He's not to know it'll be two or three weeks before the body's found, he assumes it'll be only a day or two. He goes back to the lane and looks round, tries to think of some way of establishing an alibi. He sees the stump of the tree, he thinks: I could say I was there, I was sitting there reading, I forgot the bus, that's why I was running. Now—how to back up his story? He realizes there'll be a detailed search of the area, he thinks: I could leave something at this spot that they'll be sure to trace back to me. He goes through his pockets and comes across the envelope, he thinks: That's it, I'll fold it to look like a bookmark, put it inside the tree, bed it down among the leaves where the storm wouldn't have blown it out or soaked the ink—not much use leaving it there if no one could decipher the writing.' Egan struck him as quite sharp enough for that.

'He's no murderer,' Kelsey said with finality. 'You can forget him. Now the character I'd like to know a bit more about is Derek Schofield. And George Pickthorn.' He expelled his breath in a series of little plopping sounds. Schofield and Pickthorn were both outsiders to the locality in which they now lived. Not that that need imply any inborn villainy but it might mean a past that wasn't entirely known to their present associates. Janet Marshall had thought Schofield secretive, according to Mrs Dunbar; perhaps he had something to be secretive about.

'We don't know much about either of them,' he said. He stared out of the car window at the girls walking by, cool and pretty in their summer dresses. 'I think you'd better have a little ferret round, see if you can come up with anything useful.' He glanced at his watch. 'You can drop me at the station and get started on it right away. Begin with Schofield.'

CHAPTER 14

At the bank in Market Street the manager supplied Lambert with the address of the lodgings where Schofield had been living before he moved into Ivydene. Schofield had opened his account with the bank sixteen years ago, when he first started work at the Cannonbridge Mail Order Company. He had given as one of his references the name of his previous employer, a firm called Tidman's, a wholesale grocer's in Westfleet, a small town twenty-five miles from Cannonbridge. Schofield had worked at Tidman's as a clerk since leaving school.

Lambert left the bank and went back to his car. He sat for a couple of minutes frowning out over the steering-wheel, planning his course of action: Call at Schofield's last lodgings in Cannonbridge, find out what he could there, ask if they knew Schofield's previous address, call there, and so on, tracing Schofield back through each address to his first lodgings in Cannonbridge, finding out what he could at each call. Then over to Westfleet and start the same tactics there. The whole operation would probably take him the rest of the day. He uttered a deep noisy sigh. Might as well get started, the prospect wouldn't grow any more enlivening by being delayed. He reached out and switched on the ignition.

Schofield's last lodgings were in a dismal quarter of Cannonbridge, a terrace house in a side-street two hundred yards from a small engineering works. But the house seemed reasonably well cared for, the windows clean, with presentable curtains, the exterior paintwork good for another couple of years.

Lambert pressed the bell and a few moments later the door was opened by a plump, good-natured housewife; a smell of fresh baking floated appetizingly out into the street. As soon as Lambert laid eyes on the woman he knew she was the type to chat easily and without suspicion, ramble happily on without asking questions herself.

And as soon as she clapped eyes on Lambert he saw that she knew him for a policeman. So he immediately declared himself, wondered if she might be able to help him. He was trying to trace a Mr Derek Scurfield, he understood she'd had a lodger of that name fairly recently.

'No, not Scurfield,' she said at once. 'I did have a Mr Schofield, Derek Schofield.'

Lambert allowed himself to look puzzled, disconcerted. Might he perhaps come inside and pursue the matter a little further, make sure there hadn't been some mistake over the name?

Five minutes later he was sitting at the kitchen table drinking excellent tea and despatching warm scones thickly buttered and well laced with home-made strawberry jam.

The woman chatted away in a friendly fashion. Her husband was employed as a fitter at the engineering works up the road, they had always let a room to help with the rates and the fuel bills. She gave Schofield a very good character — neat, clean, orderly, quiet, paid his rent punctually, didn't come in late, didn't smoke or drink. She had been very sorry to lose him. He had never brought a girl round to the house, she was astounded when he told her he was getting married.

'He certainly doesn't sound like our man, he's a right villain,' Lambert said, cheerfully demolishing the character of the mythical and invaluable Scurfield who popped up under various names and in different guises on many of Lambert's enquiries.

'The fellow we're after used to live at Lineholt,' he added, plucking a town at random from the air. 'He came to live in Cannonbridge about twelve months ago.'

'That settles it then,' the woman said, smiling. 'Your villain couldn't possibly be my Mr Schofield. He was with me here for three years, and before that he lodged with a very respectable widow in the next street.' He had been with the widow for eight years, had left when the widow died and her house was put up for sale. 'He was never in any kind of trouble there,' she said with energy. 'I knew his landlady well — that was how he came to lodge here, after she died.'

She wrinkled her brow. 'Before that he was in digs two streets away, over the corner shop.' She'd been in and out of the shop for the last twenty-five years, she would certainly have heard if Schofield had been in any trouble there. 'You can ask anyone in this neighbourhood,' she said with confidence. 'They'll all tell you the same, he's never been in any trouble round here.'

And before Schofield had come to Cannonbridge he'd lived, not in Lineholt, but in Westfleet. She remembered him telling her that when they'd had a little chat when he first came to lodge with her. Not that he talked much about his life in Westfleet, in fact she could never remember him mentioning the town again. 'Westfleet's not much of a place,' she said, pulling down the corners of her mouth. 'Dead and alive hole. I don't wonder he left it.'

Lambert finished his last scone, drank his last mouthful of tea and went back to his car. If there's anything to be found it'll be found over in Westfleet, he thought as he set the car in motion. Schofield couldn't have been much more than twenty when he left there. He'd been born and brought up there, had begun his working life there. Why had he all at once upped sticks and moved twenty-five miles away? Certainly not in search of adventure. He had left one clerical job for another, and his existence in bedsits, with its catalogue of early nights and sober living, seemed to have little connection with the adventurous life.

He reached a crossroads and turned the car in the direction of Westfleet; forty minutes later he was running through the suburbs. Westfleet was an uneasy amalgam of an old market town and a Victorian manufacturing addition which had now slipped into stagnation and unemployment—though sixteen years ago when Schofield had packed his bags to leave, it had been thriving and energetic, had looked forward with lively confidence to the future, was busy pulling down its cinemas and milk bars, erecting supermarkets and blocks of flats.

The old part of Westfleet was usually characterized by a somnolent decaying charm but today was market day and it had for the moment a more cheerful and bustling air, like a corpse temporarily galvanized into a semblance of life. Tidman's was situated in the old quarter and kept about its premises an atmosphere of solidity, wholesome worth and honest endeavour, deriving from its semi-rural past. The firm was still in business though the manager shook his head more than once as he talked to Lambert about the current state of trade in the town and the bleak outlook for many local firms.

Lambert had no need here to dissemble in his enquiries so he asked in a direct fashion if the manager could recall a Derek Schofield who had once worked at Tidman's. Could he supply the address where Schofield had lived at that time?

The manager didn't himself recall the name as he had been with the firm only for the last ten years, but he was able to produce the address from records: Schofield had lodged with a Mrs Wilshaw at 14 Brindley Street. And a word with a foreman who had been at Tidman's in Schofield's day revealed that Schofield had never been in any kind of trouble during his time there, had always worked diligently and unobtrusively. As to why he had decided to leave, no one could now recall—if they had ever known or cared.

Brindley Street was a few minutes' drive from Tidman's, and No. 14 was the last house in an eighteenth-century terrace that the local council had modernized some years ago after a mighty battle about whether or nor it should be pulled down. The house looked in good order now, considering its age. The curtains were bright and clean, and Lambert could see a vase of flowers at a downstairs window.

The door was opened by a tall thin woman with a sallow skin criss-crossed with fine wrinkles, and hair that looked as if it had just been resolutely waved and tinted at the hairdresser's. It was a deep chestnut brown with no trace of grey, although Lambert put the woman's age at somewhere in the early fifties.

'Mrs Wilshaw?' he asked and she gave a single nod. She had a weary, resigned air as if she didn't expect much of life but intended nevertheless to keep soldiering on; her green-brown eyes had a stubborn, unsmiling look. She didn't speak but stood waiting for him to disclose his purpose.

He decided to dispense with the services of the mythical Scurfield. He revealed his identity and asked if Mrs Wilshaw had had a lodger—a Mr Derek Schofield—some sixteen years ago. As soon as he uttered the name he knew that he had found whatever it was that Schofield had left Westfleet to escape. Her head came sharply up and she stood looking at him for a moment without replying.

'Is it the letters?' she said at last. 'I warned Madge not to write to him.'

'I think I'd better come inside,' Lambert said. She gave him another slow look and then stood aside for him to enter.

The tiny hall smelt fresh and clean. She opened a door and showed him into a little sitting-room pleasantly scented with lavender polish. She didn't offer him any refreshments but sat upright on the edge of a straight-backed chair with her hands folded tightly in her lap, waiting for him to speak. He asked her again if Schofield had lodged there sixteen or seventeen years ago.

Yes, he had lodged there for something over twelve months, he had come there shortly after his father died. And yes, it would be about seventeen years ago.

'My daughter meant no harm by the letters,' she said. 'I warned her they could cause trouble.'

The back door opened and someone came briskly in. A girl's voice called out, 'Grandma!' in a high clear tone.

Mrs Wilshaw glanced at Lambert. 'That's my grand-daughter, Gail,' she said. 'She's been wheeling out a baby from up the road.' She crossed the room and opened the door. 'I'm in here!' she called back and a few moments later Gail came along the passage.

'I'm just going to look in at Mrs Taylor's,' she said as she came. 'To see if she wants anything.' She suddenly caught sight of Lambert through the open door of the sitting-room. She halted, glancing from Lambert to her grandmother and back again. She was as tall as her grandmother, with the same very slender figure. She had light brown hair with a strong natural crimp, and her eyes—when she turned them again on Lambert with a look of enquiry—were large and brown. Lambert knew those eyes, that hair.

Schofield's eyes. And Schofield's hair.

CHAPTER 15

'This gentleman's called on a business matter,' Mrs Wilshaw said. 'Nothing important.'

Gail made a little movement of her head. 'Mrs Taylor might need some shopping,' she said. 'I won't be long.' She turned and went off again down the passage and Lambert heard the back door open and close.

He glanced round the room. On the sideboard stood a framed studio portrait, two women seated with a child between them. The child was clearly Gail four or five years ago, the older woman Mrs Wilshaw; the younger woman strongly resembled her.

'Is that your daughter?' Lambert asked.

'Yes, that's Madge, Gail's mother. She's down at the

market today, she works on a greengrocer's stall.'

'About the letters,' Lambert said.

She clasped her hands together and began to work the fingers in and out of each other. 'I'd better explain how she came to write to him,' she said. 'She couldn't see what else to do, she had to get in touch with him to tell him what Gail had decided about staying on at school, see if he'd be willing to go on paying. It meant another year at school. She wants to be a nurse, she's always wanted that, right from when she was a child, she's got her mind set on it. Madge spoke to her teacher and it seems Gail can take a course at the Tech when she leaves school, then she should be able to get into a hospital to start her training.' She moved her head. 'But of course she has to be fed and clothed and it all takes money.' She drew a long breath. 'Mr Schofield's always paid up for her as regular as clockwork.'

'How does the money come?' Lambert asked.

'In notes, through the post, every Monday morning.' She looked earnestly at him. 'Of course he always understood he'd be finished paying when she was sixteen, that was what we all agreed at the time, it seemed the usual thing. We never took him to court, none of us wanted that, we settled it between ourselves.'

She frowned. 'We never had his address after he left here. He wouldn't give us an address, he said we wouldn't need it, he'd pay without having to be chased. And Madge said to me: It'll be all right, Mum, I trust him. Well, as I said, he paid up every week and every so often he used to increase the amount off his own bat—keeping up with the cost of living, as you might say.' He'd have to do that, Lambert thought, if he wanted to avoid any sort of direct approach from the Wilshaws, any attempt to contact an employer or the courts.

'He's been very good about it,' Mrs Wilshaw said. 'I'll give him that. But then I never did have anything against him, it could happen to anyone. He was just a lad, no age really, when he came here. He was lonely and Madge was only sixteen. His mother had cleared off when he was a kid, she went off with another man, left him and his father to it, it couldn't have been much of a life for him.'

'There was no question of his marrying your daughter?' Lambert asked.

She shook her head with energy. 'No, they didn't want it, either of them, and I wasn't one to try and push it, I've never seen much good come of that.' She looked down at the carpet. 'I was married myself once. I was very young. He married me when I got pregnant with Madge, my parents forced him to marry me. He didn't want it and I didn't want it either when I saw he didn't. But my Dad threatened to take a horsewhip to him. He would have done too, he was a right Tartar.' She sighed. 'For two pins he'd have taken a horsewhip to me.'

She sighed again. 'Anyway, my husband left me after a couple of years—and they weren't happy years either. I never had a penny out of him after that, to bring Madge up. I never knew where he went, I don't even know if he's alive or dead.' She shook her head. 'I couldn't see any point in forcing that on Madge—or on Derek either, come to that.'

'The letters,' Lambert said.

'Oh yes. Well, Madge wanted to get in touch with him, to let him know he'd have to keep on paying for Gail a bit longer. She was sure he wouldn't object, it was just a question of getting hold of him—she couldn't think how to set about it. And then just by chance, one day in the spring, I saw an announcement in the local paper, the county gazette. I was looking at it in the kitchen while I was waiting for the kettle to boil. I ran straight upstairs and showed it to Madge. It was an announcement of his marriage. I knew it was him because it gave his full name, Derek Winston Schofield. It didn't give his address but it gave the bride's: Ivydene, Hadleigh, Cannonbridge. Madge said: That sounds a pretty posh sort of address, he must have done well for himself.'

She glanced sharply at Lambert. 'Not that Madge grudged him anything, and she wasn't thinking of trying anything on either, she only wanted what was due to Gail. When she said she was going to write to him at this Hadleigh address, I didn't like it. I thought: there's his new wife, I doubt if he's told her anything about Madge and Gail. I certainly didn't want any trouble — what good would that do any of us? But Madge would have it she was going to write, she'd be very careful, she'd put Private and Personal, Please Forward, on the envelope, and then the bride's family could send it on to wherever he was living.'

'Did he reply?' Lambert asked.

'Not at first. A week went by and Madge didn't hear anything. I said to her: They'll be away on their honeymoon, leave it for a bit, he won't want to find a letter from you lying on the mat the moment he gets back. But she wouldn't be put off. She said her letter must have gone astray in the post and she'd have to write again. And she did. She got a reply a few days later. He said it would be all right about Gail staying on at school, and he'd keep on with the money, but Madge wasn't to write to him again, ever, for any reason at all, they'd agreed there shouldn't be any contact and he expected her to stick to the agreement.' She frowned. 'And she wouldn't have written again but a few months after that the money suddenly stopped coming. That was the first time that had ever happened.'

'When was that?'

'Some time in June. Madge waited a few weeks, she kept thinking it would come or else he'd send some explanation. Or he might be away on his holidays and hadn't been able to attend to it. But it didn't come and he didn't write, so in the end she told me she was going to write again. I tried to tell her not to, I said perhaps he was ill, in hospital. Or he could be in some difficulties, just temporary, he could have had a lot of expense over his marriage. After all, we didn't know what his circumstances were, and he'd been very good all those years, never let her down. But she wouldn't listen, she said if he didn't want her to write, then he should have sent a letter himself, explaining. She said she needed the money and if she let it go, then he might think he could get away with not paying, and now he'd got a wife he'd probably prefer to spend the money on her rather than on a daughter he'd never seen.'

'He's never seen Gail?' Lambert said.

She shook her head but didn't enlarge. 'So Madge wrote again and this time she got a letter back right away. She didn't show me the letter, seeing I'd been so against her writing, she just said it was all right, he'd be sending the money. And sure enough it did come quite soon afterwards.'

'I'd like those dates,' Lambert said. 'When the letters were written, when she got the replies, when he paid off what was owing, and so on.'

'I'm afraid you'll have to ask my daughter all that—if you want the dates exact, that is, I could only give you a rough idea.'

'Did you ever write to Schofield yourself?' Lambert asked suddenly.

'Me?' she said with astonishment. 'No! Whatever would I do that for?'

'Or to anyone else?' he persisted. 'Any relative of Schofield's? His sister-in-law, for instance?'

She stared at him. 'Of course not! Whatever gave you such an idea? I don't know anything about any sister-in-law.' She frowned. 'What has he been telling you?' She seemed to be under the impression that Schofield had made a complaint to the police.

'I don't know what he's told you,' she said with some agitation, 'but Madge never tried to blackmail him, you must believe that. I know it might look like that with him just getting married, but it wasn't like that at all, Madge isn't that kind of woman.'

'I'm sure she's not,' Lambert said. 'I'll just have a word with your daughter, get it all cleared up, then you can rest easy in your mind.'

She looked relieved. 'Oh yes, if you would, I'd be very glad. You'll easily spot Madge at the market. They won't be so busy now, not at this time of the afternoon, she'll be able to have a word with you. It's Braithwaite's where she works, the biggest greengrocer's stall, you can't miss it, they've got a board up with the name.' She nodded over at the photograph. 'You'll recognize her all right.' She glanced anxiously at him. 'You won't—'

'Don't worry,' he said. 'I'll make sure no one else knows what my business is.'

She came with him to the front door. 'I work in the evenings,' she said. 'Washing up in a café. I've done it for years.' She smiled faintly. 'That's how Gail came to be born.' She watched him walk off down the street and turn the corner to where he had left his car parked discreetly out of sight.

As he laid his fingers on the door-handle he saw Gail come into view at the other end of the street, carrying a shopping-bag. He stood waiting till she came up. She walked well, with a rangy, springy step. She was a pleasant-looking girl, pretty enough in a fresh, wholesome way; her crimped hair gave her a fashionable look. She smiled as she recognized him, she had a friendly, unaffected air.

She halted by the car. 'You've finished your business with Grandma?' she said as if she took him for an insurance agent. She smiled. 'It's such a lovely afternoon,

I'm going to take Miss Johnstone out in her wheelchair as soon as I've dropped this bag in at Mrs Taylor's.' She saw his look of enquiry. 'Miss Johnstone was knocked down by a car a few years ago. She used to be in a State home but she couldn't bear it, so she came out again. She hasn't got any relatives, she lives in lodgings in the next street, the landlady's very good to her. I go round there in the evenings during the school terms but in the holidays I go during the day as well. She likes that, she enjoys being wheeled out in the daytime, it's a bit more lively.'

'You seem to like looking after people,' Lambert said.

'Yes, I do.' She grinned. 'When I was a kid I never bothered with dolls, I used to help with all the babies round here.'

'Your grandmother tells me you're going to be a nurse.'

'Yes, as soon as I leave school, I'm looking forward to that.' She seemed shut up safe and tight inside her cocoon of purpose and determination. She'd found out what she was going to do, was working her way steadily towards it, unshakable, set fair, it seemed.

He didn't tell her he was going to the market to speak to her mother. He didn't know how much she'd been told about her father, how much she cared; he didn't even know what surname she went by. Certainly it seemed to have produced a fair result, a household of females.

'I wish you luck with the nursing,' he said. 'I'm certain you'll do well.' She smiled at him with Schofield's eyes but without Schofield's look of habitual anxiety; her glance was optimistic, level and confident.

He watched her as she set off again with her shopping-bag, springy and resolute. A pity Schofield never met her, he thought, he might have been proud of her.

The market consisted of twenty or thirty stalls set up in a square in the old part of Westfleet. Braithwaite's was easy to find with its large painted sign, its blackboard of chalked prices, mounds of tomatoes and cucumbers, skips of mushrooms, punnets of blackberries.

Madge—Wilshaw, I suppose, Lambert thought, she didn't appear ever to have married—was serving in the middle of the stall. She looked older than her photograph, she wore a sleeveless cotton dress and her arms and shoulders, her face and neck were all darkly tanned; her brown hair was bleached by the sun in uneven streaks. She frowned all the time, whether against the brilliant afternoon or from chronic anxiety Lambert couldn't make out.

As he approached he saw that her skin was already finely patterned with the same network of lines he had seen etched on her mother's face but in addition she had two lines of her own deeply scored between her brows. She couldn't be more than thirty-three or four but she looked a good forty.

She glanced up at Lambert as she handed change to a customer. She wore grimed rubber gloves to deal with the fruit and vegetables. 'Yes?' She looked at him from her mother's eyes, green-brown, unsmiling.

Lambert had already decided on his purchase, a bunch of bananas from among those suspended by metal hooks from a rail that ran along under the canvas roof of the stall. He indicated the farthest bunch and followed her as she moved along to the end of the stall to reach it down. In a discreet tone he disclosed his identity and asked if she could leave the stall for a few minutes to speak to him.

She was startled for a moment but recovered herself at once. She didn't ask what it was about and he had the impression that she believed she knew. She flashed him a wary, anxious look. 'You've no need to alarm yourself,' he said. 'I just need some information.' He told her he'd already spoken to her mother and all he needed was confirmation of some details. He still didn't say what about.

'All right,' she said and went off to speak to the man in charge of the stall. He was busy dealing with a pernickety customer and he gave Madge no more than a quick abstracted nod, he didn't glance at Lambert. 'It's OK,' she said when she came back. 'But I mustn't be long. We can go over there.' She jerked her head at a nearby patch of waste ground. She walked quickly off and he followed her.

'It's about your recent correspondence with Mr Derek Schofield,' he said when they came to a halt. She gave a little nod. 'I've talked it over with your mother,' he added. 'There's no need for you to worry, we're quite satisfied.' This vague assurance seemed to soothe her, he saw her relax slightly.

'I meant no harm,' she said, spikily defensive.

'No, of course not, we understand that. If I could just check one or two details, then we can forget about it.' She nodded again, anxious to satisfy him, to get back to the stall.

Yes, she could remember the correspondence clearly. She had written the first two letters in April; her third and last letter was written in July. She had posted it on a Saturday morning, that would be July 19th, she could remember that because it was two days before her mother's birthday and she had bought a card in the post office at the same time as she posted the letter. 'I don't write that many letters,' she said. 'Not enough to get mixed up about them.'

'What address did you put on that last letter?' Lambert asked.

'The same as on the other two, care of Ivydene. I don't know where he's been living since he got married but I thought for sure his wife's family must know.' When Schofield replied he didn't put any address at the head of his letter. He'd answered almost at once, on the following Wednesday—that would be July 23rd. He was full of apologies, he'd had a number of unforeseen expenses, he'd do what he could about the arrears as soon as possible. On no account whatever was she to write again; this was heavily underlined.

Ten days later, on a Friday—making it August 1st—she got half of what was owing and on the following Friday, August 8th, the remainder came. Last Monday—August 18th—the weekly money had arrived again in the usual way and she expected it to continue like this.

'Did you ever in any of your letters,' Lambert said, 'make any kind of threat? Say you'd tell his wife or his employer, or make any other kind of threat?' She began to shake her head but he went on: 'You needn't be afraid that some action will be taken against you if you tell me now that you did make some such threat—it would be easy to understand if you did. I'm anxious to know the truth about this.'

She shook her head decisively. 'No, I did not.'

'You're absolutely sure?'

'Yes, I'm sure.'

'You'd swear to that?'

She gave him a startled look.

'It's the truth?' he persisted. 'You could swear to it?'

'Yes, I could.' she said after a moment. 'It's the truth.'

'Did you write to anyone else on this matter?'

She looked mystified. 'Who else would I write to?'

'To his wife, perhaps.'

'Good heavens, no! I wouldn't do such a thing!'

'Or some other relative?'

She looked baffled. 'I don't know of any other relative.'

'In-laws perhaps?' Lambert said. 'His sister-in-law, for instance?'

'I don't know any sister-in-law,' she said with an edge of anger in her tone. 'And I wouldn't have written to her if I did. What would be the point of that?'

'Did your mother write to Schofield—or to any member

of his family—about any of this?'

'No, she did not!' she answered with force. 'She was dead against me writing to Derek in the first place.'

'Did anyone ever call at your house, making any kind of enquiry about Schofield? Asking if he'd lodged there?'

She drew a long, exasperated breath. No, there had never been anything like that. Nor had she ever received any letter enquiring about him.

'You'd swear to all that?' he said again.

She closed her eyes for an instant. 'Yes, I would.'

'That's about it then,' he said. 'I don't think you'll hear any more of this.' He thanked her for her co-operation and she went swiftly off with an air of profound relief.

A clock above a jeweller's showed twenty minutes to four as Lambert crossed the square on his way to the car park—and Cannonbridge. He glanced back at the stall and saw that she was already at work again, her blue rubber hands darting and swooping among the melons and courgettes.

CHAPTER 16

'We'll have Schofield in right away,' Kelsey said. 'Give him a ring now, you'll catch him before he leaves work.'

Over the phone Schofield's voice sounded tense and brittle. 'I'll be at the station in fifteen minutes,' he told Lambert.

And bang on time he was shown into Kelsey's office. The Chief didn't beat about the bush. 'We've been ferreting about in your past,' he said briskly. 'We know about your daughter.'

Schofield closed his eyes and drew a little sighing breath.

'One or two questions this gives rise to,' Kelsey said.

Schofield's eyes jerked open. 'You're not going to tell Lisa?' he said on a note of panic.

Kelsey moved his shoulders. 'We certainly won't go out of our way to tell her. But that's not to say it won't come out in the course of all this—one way or another.' If you killed Janet Marshall, my lad, he thought grimly, you'll find you've got no secrets left from anyone. And if you didn't kill her . . . Five years, Carole Gardiner said, licking the cream and jam from her ripe lips, in five years it'll be a different story with Lisa and Schofield.

He picked up a pen and began to seesaw it between his fingers. 'Madge Wilshaw saw the announcement of your marriage in the paper. She wrote you two letters—'

'No, not two letters,' Schofield interrupted, then he stopped and frowned. 'You're right,' he added after a moment. 'She did write two, but the first one went astray, I never got it. She mentioned that in the letter I did get, she said she'd already written and got no reply.'

'I'm suggesting,' Kelsey said, 'that the first letter did not go astray. You and Lisa were away on your honeymoon when that letter arrived at Ivydene, it's quite possible that Janet opened it and read it.'

'Oh no!' Schofield said at once. 'Janet would never do that. She was the last person in the world to open a letter addressed to someone else.'

'In the ordinary way I'm sure you're right,' Kelsey said. 'But if the letter was addressed to the man who had just married her young sister, very much against her own wishes, a man of whom she knew little, then she might feel it was her plain duty to open the letter, see if she could discover anything from it—particularly if the envelope was marked Private and Personal.' He rapped his pen on the desk. 'And if she did open it, then she did indeed learn something from its contents.'

Schofield put up a hand and massaged his cheek. 'She never said anything to me about the letter—I don't

believe she read it. She'd have told Lisa what she'd found
out the moment we got back from Tangier.'

'I can't agree with you there,' Kelsey said equably.
'Janet was on the point of leaving Ivydene when the letter
arrived. She was making the move without a word to you
or Lisa, that surely argues an angry, hostile, even
vindictive state of mind. When she read the letter she
could have thought: Serve Lisa right if this is the kind of
husband she's got for herself, I wish her joy of him, she
needn't come crying to me when she finds out what he's
really like, I'm washing my hands of her.'

Schofield stared down at a patch of sunlight on the
carpet.

'But time passes,' Kelsey said, 'and Janet simmers
down. She likes her new job, her mind is no longer so
much on Lisa. And Lisa is anxious to be friends again,
she keeps pressing Janet to go over to Ivydene. Janet may
begin to think: After all, Lisa's very young, my mother
did leave her in my care, perhaps it isn't right to wash my
hands of her. Janet's not sure what she ought to do or
what she can do. Perhaps she decided to put an enquiry
agent on to you, see if there was anything else to be
discovered.' He threw down his pen. 'Or perhaps she
decided to tackle you face to face about your past.'

'She never spoke to me about it,' Schofield said again.

Kelsey ignored the statement. 'Lisa was pressing her
about the holidays. But how could she go to Ivydene,
knowing what she knew, and not say anything about it to
Lisa? How could she stay a week or a fortnight in the
house, with Lisa chattering on, asking her advice and so
on, and keep her mouth shut about what she knew? She
would feel deceitful, ill at ease, it would be an impossible
situation for her. But the end of term was coming and she
had to make up her mind.'

Kelsey leaned forward. 'Lisa is under the impression
that Janet didn't answer her last letter. But I suggest that

Janet did answer it — by writing to you. You are always downstairs first in the morning, you always pick up the post.'

'She didn't write to me,' Schofield said.

Kelsey stood up and walked about. 'I will put to you a possible course of events,' he said in a tone of detached reasoning, like a lecturer addressing students. 'In her letter Janet asked you to go over to Rose Cottage, there was something she must speak to you about, something she had discovered. You had a pretty good idea what that something might be. You fixed yourself a day off work, you arranged one of your sore throats, you took good care no one knew you were going over to Longmead.'

'Not a word of that's true,' Schofield said with protest. 'I didn't go over there.'

Kelsey stabbed a finger at the air. 'We will further suppose that when you got to Rose Cottage Janet confronted you with the letter from Madge Wilshaw which she'd kept ever since she'd read it at Easter. You were horrified, you had to get the letter back from her, you had to destroy it. You had to silence Janet.'

'No,' Schofield said. 'No, no, no.' He dropped his head into his hands.

'You were in some financial difficulty before Janet's death,' Kelsey said. 'How were you proposing to deal with it?'

'I kept juggling the bills,' Schofield said in a muffled tone from between his hands. 'I just did the best I could.'

'Janet's death has been of considerable benefit to you. Your financial worries are over, you now have access to a substantial sum of money. You are in possession of Ivydene, you can do what Lisa wants, sell the house and move. And you are rid of a hostile sister-in-law who was always a threat to your marriage.'

Schofield raised his head. 'That doesn't mean I killed her. She never once mentioned my daughter to me, she never even hinted she knew about Gail or Madge. I don't believe she did.' His voice trailed off, he sat trembling and shaken.

'Do you possess a key to Rose Cottage?' Kelsey asked suddenly.

Schofield jerked his head up. 'No, of course not. Why would I have a key?'

'Has your wife a key to the cottage?'

'No, of course she hasn't.'

'Has either of your ever had a key?'

'No, never.' Schofield's look was alert now and wary, every line of his body expressed controlled tension.

Kelsey sat looking at him in silence for several seconds, then he said abruptly, 'Better get off home.' Schofield didn't need telling twice.

'Get on to the local enquiry agents,' Kelsey said to Lambert as soon as the door had closed behind Schofield. 'See if Janet did put anyone on to him.' Even if she hadn't intercepted the letter frcm Madge Wilshaw she could have decided there was something fishy about Schofield and it might be an idea to have enquiries made. She could have discovered the existence of Brindley Street and the Wilshaws all by herself.

Lambert set smartly off next morning to see what he could discover about George Pickthorn. 'Look sharp about it,' Kelsey said. 'I want to pop out to Mayfield Farm, see if we can get a word with the four of them together, dinner-time would be the best for that.'

Lambert knew little about Pickthorn's life before he moved to Longmead. He knew the name of the Cannon-bridge firm where Pickthorn had worked till his retirement five years ago—Sadgrove's in Blackmore Road—but he didn't know Pickthorn's old address in Cannonbridge, nor did he have the name of Pickthorn's bank. He decided to go along first to Sadgrove's.

It was a sizable firm, established fifty years ago in premises that had since been extended and modernized. The manager was an energetic, youngish man who'd been with the firm only a couple of years. He didn't know George Pickthorn and he didn't ask why the sergeant needed his old address. But in the couple of minutes he felt able to devote to Lambert he instructed a clerk to look up the information in the records.

In another few minutes Lambert had the answer: No. 5 Moreland Street. He knew the district, on the eastern edge of town. He drove over there at once, parked his car round the corner and walked to No. 5. It was a middle house in a terrace that had been modernized piecemeal with haphazard and occasionally startling results, bay windows sprouting unexpectedly, reproduction Georgian doors of offensive newness, do-it-yourself porches in unashamedly synthetic materials, front doors in a medley of brilliant and unrelated hues.

Lambert rang the bell. There was no answer. He rang again, a third and yet a fourth time; still no answer. He stood irresolute, then he turned away and began to walk slowly up the street, pondering his next move.

A woman came briskly towards him. 'They're away,' she called out to Lambert as she approached. 'The Bartletts, I saw you ring their bell. They're on holiday in Bournemouth, they won't be back for another week. I'm their next-door neighbour.' She was a tall, well-built, rather smart woman in her late fifties, not bad-looking for her age. She had a great deal of thick wavy hair of a shade never encountered in nature but which Lambert often noticed in smartish sexyish middle-aged women. He wondered sometimes how or why the manufacturers had hit upon that particular shade, a cross between mahogany and stewed damson, but they must have known their business for it certainly seemed popular. He had once eaten lunch in a restaurant run by a local council where every single waitress had sported locks of that same strange hue. It had given him indigestion trying to work out how that could possibly have come about—surely not by municipal decree?—and the odds against its happening entirely by chance.

'I wanted to enquire about a Mr George Pickthorn,' he said. 'I believe he used to live at No. 5.'

'That's right.' She made a little dismissive gesture. 'But that was three or four years ago. The Bartletts couldn't tell you anything about him, they've only lived in the house twelve months. The people that bought it off Mr Pickthorn moved to Ellenborough.'

She levelled a frank, assessing glance at him, his shoulders, grooming, general air. 'You're a copper,' she said. He moved his head in acquiescence.

'Is it about children?' she said. 'Has he done something to a child?'

CHAPTER 17

'I think I'd better come inside,' Lambert said. 'And talk to you.'

She pulled a little face. 'Oh—all right then. I'll put the kettle on, I'm dying for a cup of tea.' She took a key from her bag and opened the door, talking all the while to him over her shoulder. 'Mrs Randall said to me: What do you think? Should we go to the police? But in the end we didn't do anything. I'd only been living here three or four months at that time and Mr Pickthorn hadn't long lost his wife. It would have been a fine way to start off round here, accusing a neighbour of God knows what.'

The narrow hall was dazzlingly furnished with a crimson carpet in a large floral pattern, gaily-coloured wallpaper and a pendant light fitting in wrought iron of excruciating complexity. Lambert had to duck to avoid running himself through the skull on its more spiky projections.

She kicked off her shoes and walked ahead of him into the kitchen. The walls were covered with a vinyl paper in a jazzy pattern of vast fruit and vegetables in brilliant and improbable colours. He wondered fleetingly if she ever suffered from migraine. She picked up a pair of slippers, sat down and pulled them on. 'Oh—that's better!' She blew out a strong breath of relief. 'My feet play me up in this weather.'

She stood up and crossed to the sink, she ran water into the kettle. 'Are you hungry?' she asked as she set the kettle on the stove. She took down a tin from the dresser. 'I didn't have any breakfast myself, I'm ravenous.' She pulled out a number of plastic bags from the tin. 'Go on, dig in, I get these from work, they're quite fresh, I brought this lot home yesterday.' She saw his look. 'It's all quite legal. We can help ourselves from the reject bins.' She worked part-time at a little factory on the industrial estate, packing snacks for sale in pubs and discos; nuts, raisins, pork scratchings, potato puffs, cheese savouries. Lambert dug in as instructed. They were all quite tasty, a curious mixture, tempting, unsatisfying.

'Not bad, are they?' she said as she took another handful. She'd just come over on the bus from the other side of town, she'd spent the night with her married daughter. 'Her husband's away on business,' she explained. 'She gets nervous on her own with the kids, she likes me to go over there to spend the evening, stay the night.'

'You knew Mr Pickthorn?' Lambert said as she reached down cups and saucers.

'No, not really. I lived in Hayford before I came to Cannonbridge. I only moved here after my husband died, to be near my daughter. Mrs Pickthorn died a couple of months before I bought this house and Mr Pickthorn was keeping pretty much to himself. I could understand that, it was only eighteen months since I'd lost my husband, it takes time to get over these things. I saw him about, of course, we passed the time of day, but that was all. Then my daughter had to go into hospital and I took the twins for a few weeks — it was the summer holidays, I hadn't started my job then.' She'd sent the twins off to the park every day, they were eight years old at that time, a boy and a girl.

'And Mr Pickthorn talked to them in the park?' Lambert hazarded. 'His behaviour worried you?'

'No, not me, I didn't know anything about it.' The kettle boiled and she made the tea. 'It was this Mrs Randall. She came up to me one day in a shop. I had the twins with me and she recognized them from the park. She said: I hope you don't mind me speaking to you but I go to the Memorial Park quite a lot and I've seen your grandchildren there. They'd told her about their mother being in hospital and that they were staying with me. Mrs Randall said to me: It's Mr Pickthorn I want to speak to you about, the children tell me he's your neighbour.

'She said he was hanging round the children in the park and it worried her. He hadn't specially singled out my grandchildren, it was just whatever children were there. I asked her if he spoke to them or offered them sweets, but she said no, not as far as she'd seen. She's one of those chatty old ladies, I didn't know if she might not have fancied the whole thing; being lonely, she could have made it up to create a bit of excitement. And for all I knew she could have had some grudge against Mr Pickthorn, she might have been trying to get him into trouble.' She poured out the tea.

'Anyway, we talked it over and I didn't quite know what to make of it. Mrs Randall thought perhaps we ought to go to the police but I wasn't keen.'

'So what did you do?' Lambert asked. He drank his tea and helped himself to another handful of nutty nibbles.

'I stopped the twins going to the Memorial Park and I stopped them going anywhere on their own. I started taking them to the Jubilee Gardens myself and I kept more of an eye on them all round. And they were only with me another ten days after that. Then Mr Pickthorn suddenly put his house up for sale and moved away, into the country somewhere. He did tell me where, when he was leaving, but I'm afraid I've forgotten.'

'Do you know where Mrs Randall lives?' Lambert asked.

'Yes, in one of those old houses over by the Memorial Park, opposite the park gates. There's a big butterfly bush in the front garden.'

Lambert stood up. He thanked her for her help and then swung into one of his standard spiels. 'I must emphasize that Mr Pickthorn is not in trouble, there is no charge of any kind against him.' He could tell she was a woman of discretion, the way she had behaved over the episode of the children three or four years ago would have told him that even if he hadn't had the pleasure of talking to her. She looked pleased, and smiled at him. Eight years ago when Lambert was a fledgling detective-constable over at the other side of the county, there had been an elderly woman suspected of theft at the hotel where she worked in the linen room. The police—among them Lambert—made enquiries at the hotel and the woman hanged herself. It turned out later that the thefts had been the work of one of the chambermaids. Lambert had never forgotten the case.

'I know you'll keep all this to yourself,' he added. 'We don't want to run the risk of injuring the reputation of a perfectly innocent man.' He gave her a level look. 'We'd none of us relish that happening to us.' He had no idea if this ploy had any effect but it always seemed to be well received—and he had never had any better inspiration.

She looked back at him with a reflective, half-startled gaze. 'No, by God we wouldn't,' she said with fervour. 'You can rely on me. Mum's the word.'

The buddleia in Mrs Randall's front garden was a fine large specimen with long flowering spikes of a soft shade of lilac. The house was a substantial Edwardian villa with the slightly seedy air of a dwelling belonging to an old woman who no longer has a husband to do odd jobs, or enough money to pay someone else to keep the property in repair.

Mrs Randall took some time to answer the door after Lambert pressed the bell but he stood waiting without impatience; he could hear a radio playing, and after a few moments, the sound of slow movement inside the house. He stood glancing about at the garden, a widow's garden, the earth in the forlorn flowerbeds rock hard in the summer heat, discouraged perennials straggling along the sour borders, weeds flourishing unchecked in the gravel paths, the hedges shooting upwards and outwards, ragged and unrestrained.

The door opened and a stooping old woman peered out at him. She gave him a smile of cheerful apology. 'I'm afraid it takes me a long time to get to the door these days.' He saw that she was leaning on a stick.

He introduced himself and told her he was making enquiries about a Mr George Pickthorn, he'd been over to Moreland Street and spoken to the lady next door; she had referred him to Mrs Randall.

She opened the door wide. 'Do come in,' she said. 'You can't stand talking out there.' He gave her his arm and they went into a sitting-room, large and comfortably furnished, with chintz curtains fluttering at the windows and a canary singing in a cage.

'It'll be about that business with the children,' she said

as they sat down. 'Has he been in trouble again?'

'He wasn't in trouble before, as far as I know,' Lambert said amiably.

She moved her head. 'No, I suppose not, not officially, anyway.' She gave him a shrewd glance. 'But he must be mixed up in something or you wouldn't be here now, asking questions. And the only dealings I've had with the lady next door to him in Moreland Street was that business three or four years ago about the children.'

'He's not in any trouble,' Lambert repeated. 'I'm making general enquiries which may turn out to have nothing whatever to do with Mr Pickthorn.'

She looked relieved if somewhat baffled. 'Oh good,' she said. 'I'm glad to hear it.'

'But I would like to know about that business of the children,' he added. 'If you could just tell me what you know, I won't keep you long.'

'That's all right.' She smiled at him. 'I'm not going anywhere. To tell you the truth, I'm glad of the company. I don't get out much now, not since my accident. I slipped on the ice a couple of years back and broke my leg in two places. It's never been the same since.'

'You used to go over the road to the park before your accident?'

'Oh yes, I went there a lot. I used to sit and read the paper, have a chat, see a bit of life going on. I noticed Mr Pickthorn hanging about near the children one summer holidays. Of course at first I didn't know who he was but I found out from the children.'

'Did he do anything?' Lambert asked. 'Did he speak to them, offer them anything?'

She shook her head. 'Not that I ever saw. If one of them spoke to him he'd answer, but he didn't persist, and the children would run off again, back to their games.'

'But it disturbed you all the same?'

She looked at him from faded blue eyes, still lively and

intelligent. 'A man of sixty-odd hanging about there every day, it'd disturb anyone. What really bothered me—there had been some trouble there a few years before and I didn't want the same thing happening again. A man, quite a bit younger than Mr Pickthorn, he started talking to the children, giving them sweets and pennies. Some of the fathers got together and they beat him up.'

'Perhaps Mr Pickthorn was just lonely?' Lambert said.

She moved her head. 'Yes, I suppose that could be it, loneliness can be a terrible thing. I did try to talk to him but he wouldn't chat, he just wanted to be looking at the children.'

'I don't see any need to speak to Pickthorn,' Kelsey said. There had never been any official complaint, nothing in the files. In a murder investigation they unearthed all sorts of facts about people even remotely connected with the crime; most of the information was totally irrelevant, never made use of.

'Probably just some temporary aberration,' Kelsey said. 'Going through a bad patch.' He stroked his chin. 'Shock, loneliness, bereavement, they can play strange tricks.'

CHAPTER 18

The midday sun shone fiercely down as Sergeant Lambert drove the Chief out to Mayfield Farm. Kelsey hoped to find Oswald Slater, his wife, and Neil Fleming together for lunch; with luck Ken Bryant would also be somewhere about. He wanted to talk to all of them at the same time.

He hadn't so far spent a great deal of time talking to any of them. They had all been down at Rose Cottage when the police arrived after the discovery of Janet Marshall's body and later on that same morning he had spoken to them together at the farm.

'As far as any direct involvement in the death is concerned,' Sergeant Lambert said, 'we can surely forget all four of them.' They'd checked on Oswald Slater; he'd kept his dental appointment in Cannonbridge at four-thirty, had gone on afterwards to Jessup's farm at the other side of Cannonbridge and had stayed there till after six.

Mrs Slater had attended to her usual duties about the farm. The two workmen, Ken Bryant and Neil Fleming, were in the position of vouching for each other, having been in each other's company during all the working hours of that Friday.

There were no prints of either of the Slaters at Rose Cottage, and none of Neil Fleming's. There were a couple of Ken Bryant's on the underside of a small table in the bedroom; he told them he'd helped to lay a carpet there when Miss Marshall moved in. This was confirmed by Oswald Slater who said he'd asked Bryant to give Miss Marshall any assistance she might need during the move.

In reply to Lambert's observation Kelsey gave a non-committal grunt. On the face of it, yes, he would have agreed that they could forget Mayfield Farm — and yet there was something there that niggled at him, something he couldn't put a finger on.

As they approached Mayfield he glanced out at the farm buildings. In a field near the house a pair of snow-white goats grazed inside a stout fence newly erected and painted.

'Constable Drew tells me he's bought his turkey from Mrs Slater every Christmas for the past fifteen years,' Kelsey said as Lambert turned the car in through the gates. 'Damn good turkeys too, he says.' The constable had a passing acquaintance with the Slaters, being himself a local man.

A cautious, close-fisted type, Oswald Slater, Drew had

told the Chief, respected in local farming circles for his judgment and acumen, a good eye for beef cattle. Not a man of grandiose ideas, not avid for expansion. He'll never fall foul of his bank manager, Drew had said with certainty. And Margaret Slater was reputed locally to have as good a head for business as her husband; they pulled well in double harness.

As Kelsey got out of the car he spotted Ken Bryant coming out of the turkey sheds. He gave a shout and Bryant came over. 'I'd like you to come into the house,' Kelsey said. 'I want a word with all of you together. I won't keep you long, I know it's your dinner-time.'

Bryant went round to the back entrance as the two policemen walked up to the front door. Lambert pressed the bell and a moment later Mrs Slater admitted them.

Lambert ran his eye over her as the Chief explained their errand. Not very tall, quite trimly built, approaching middle age. An ordinary-looking sensible farmer's wife, no more related to the sergeant's notion of disturbing femininity than his landlady, the cleaners at the police station, or for that matter, seventy-five percent of the entire adult female population.

She led the way into a sitting-room pleasantly furnished in traditional country style. The two workmen came into the room a minute or two later, followed by Slater.

'I'm sure you've all discussed what's happened,' the Chief said. 'It's possible you may have remembered some further details.' No one replied.

Kelsey glanced at Slater. 'For instance, when you left the farm at four-fifteen that Friday, and drove off up the Cannonbridge road, did you happen to glance along Quarry Lane? Did you notice if there was a vehicle parked in the run-in? Or for that matter, as you came back again past Quarry Lane on your way home that evening, did you happen to glance in that direction?'

Slater thought for a moment, then he shook his head. 'I

do usually give a look down that way, to see if anything's coming,' he said, 'but I can't remember noticing the run-in that day, or seeing anything parked there.'

Kelsey glanced at the two workmen. 'Did either of your notice the run-in at any time during that day? Did you see any vehicle there?' Again there was a brief silence followed by a shaking of heads.

As the Chief took them back over old ground in the hope of jogging a memory, the niggling doubt he'd felt earlier rose sharply again in his brain. Somewhere in the room he felt a powerful sense of deception, an emanation which experience had taught him never to ignore.

As the talk jerked spasmodically on he tried to locate the source of the emanation, looking directly into the eyes of each of the four in turn.

Oswald Slater's grey eyes had a quality of granite, a solid, impenetrable look. Margaret Slater's eyes were not particularly large or well set but had a curious look of depth, he saw suddenly. He hadn't noticed them before, it was not her habit to look directly at the person to whom she spoke. Not that there was anything shifty about her gaze, but rather a deliberately lowered, averted quality as in the faces of Quaker women in old portraits. She said very little but didn't hesitate or falter when it was necessary for her to speak. As to her eyes—they were a pretty, rather unusual colour, the colour of amber, he decided after a moment, flecked with tiny gold points of light—interesting, fascinating eyes . . . He suddenly realized he was staring at her and pulled himself up with a blink.

'I walked back up to the house with Neil, just after half past six,' Ken Bryant was saying. 'Mr Slater had just driven in. I spoke to him and then I went down home. I had a meal and a read of the paper, then I went back up to the turkey sheds for an hour.' He had seen nothing going on round Rose Cottage, had heard nothing, noticed nothing in any way unusual. Brown eyes, Kelsey saw, dark and opaque under bushy brows, revealing nothing.

'That's right,' Neil Fleming confirmed. His position at Mayfield must be a little tricky, Kelsey pondered, part employee, part member of the household. Easy enough in such a situation to provoke irritation by being too pushy or too reticent; Fleming appeared to avoid both extremes. Pale blue eyes, a light, flickering gaze. His full lower lip and surviving milk tooth made him look even younger than he was.

No new information seemed forthcoming but Kelsey still felt this strong sense of deceit. He lowered his head and closed his eyes to give instinct a chance to speak.

Oswald Slater was talking about that Friday evening, recalling the fury of the storm; his voice went on, harsh and monotonous. The Chief sat with his eyes closed, waiting.

And instinct spoke at last, loud and clear. And the name it spoke was Ken Bryant.

CHAPTER 19

Kelsey rose to his feet. Slater had now come to the end of his monologue. 'I've no more questions for the moment,' Kelsey told him. He glanced at Bryant. 'But I would like another word with Jill. Would it be inconvenient if we called in now at your cottage? There are one or two further points I'd like to put to your daughter, and that's always best done in the presence of the parents.'

'Go right ahead,' Bryant said amiably. 'She'll be at home now, for her dinner.'

Bryant reached the back door of his cottage a couple of minutes before the two policemen opened his garden gate and walked up the front path. Just time for Ken to warn his wife of their coming, but the warning was no longer vitally necessary. Since Monday Mollie had taken care to dress herself at the beginning of each new—and highly interesting—day in attire fit to meet the eye of any caller.

When she opened the door now to the policemen she wore a neatly ironed blouse of some pale cream silky material and a pleated skirt the colour of canned spinach; the combined effect was rather elegant. She had made a special journey into Cannonbridge to buy a foundation lotion and a box of face powder and had used them to good effect to tone down her complexion. She had also bought a rinse that subdued her brassy locks to a pleasant shade of light chestnut, and a conditioner to quell the frizz; her hair was now drawn smoothly back into a French pleat. It was possible to discern that twenty years ago she must have been quite an eye-catcher.

She didn't seem at all put out to see the two men although she'd been just about to dish up. The kitchen was filled with the smell of roasting meat and simmering vegetables, and Jill was already sitting at the table.

But she didn't seem to mind waiting a little longer for her dinner. 'Shall I go next door and fetch Heather?' she asked Kelsey. 'Do you want to talk to her as well?'

'Yes, do that,' Kelsey said and she stood up from the table and ran off. Kelsey took out a handkerchief and dabbed at his forehead. In spite of the open window the heat in the kitchen was stifling. He could feel the sweat gathering all over his body and the sensation was powerfully unpleasant.

Mrs Bryant remained standing by the stove, apparently unaffected by the heat. 'The girls have been that upset,' she said. 'Miss Marshall took such an interest in them both. She was going to help Jill with her maths later on in the holidays.' She stirred a pan of gravy with a wooden spoon.

Jill came running back with Heather Abell who had been snatched from the middle of her dinner—not that she appeared to mind. Kelsey spent a minute or two chatting to the girls about the holidays, how they were spending them, before he got down to business. They answered readily enough but they gazed up at him with the unemotional shuttered look he had often seen in children whose lives had been brushed by tragedy or violence.

'When Miss Marshall came back to school after dinner that Friday,' Kelsey said, 'did either of you speak to her?'

Jill nodded. 'We were helping to clear the classrooms for the holidays. We were in Miss Marshall's room, taking some charts down from the wall when she came in. She was in a rush.'

'Did she say why she was late?'

Jill frowned down at the floor. 'No, she just told us to wash our hands before the bell rang.' As they talked Kelsey kept an eye on Bryant. He seemed proud of his daughter, he eyed her with approval, smiled unconsciously when she spoke. Mrs Bryant was more concerned with the state of her cooking, the kitchen, the table. She raised a pan lid from time to time, straightened a knife on the table, brushed a speck from the cloth.

'When you went next door to Rose Cottage to show Miss Marshall the kitten,' Kelsey said, 'did you see anyone in the lane? Or anyone sitting at the side of the lane?' Both girls shook their heads. 'Did you see Clive Egan?' Bryant's head jerked up at that and he gave the Chief a startled look.

'No,' the girls said again.

'Did you see—or hear—Clive running up the lane towards the crossroads?' Kelsey persisted but again they shook their heads.

I suppose they could just have missed him, he thought. Or been too absorbed in their chatter and the antics of the kitten to pay attention to anything else.

'Did Miss Marshall say anything about going away? Did she mention anyone calling at the cottage?'

'Heather was talking to her more than I was,' Jill said. 'She had to go back into school for her skipping-rope and she was talking to Miss Marshall then.'

Heather blushed at the sudden spotlight. She looked anxiously up at the Chief. 'After I found my rope I helped Miss Marshall to finish clearing up in her room. I found Stuart Hitchman's ball under a desk—'

'That red and yellow ball?' Jill said with interest. 'The one he won at the fair?'

'If we could get back to Miss Marshall,' Kelsey said, holding grimly on to his patience. Perspiration trickled down under his collar. 'Did she mention any caller?'

'I said I'd take the ball and give it to Stuart,' Heather said, unable to depart from the path on which she had embarked. 'But Miss Marshall said she'd take it. She had a lot of stuff to take home and she couldn't fit it all into her bags. I said why didn't she ask Mr Lloyd if she could borrow the basket from the exhibition in the hall. She said it was a good idea and she went off and asked him.'

Red and yellow ball, Sergeant Lambert thought. He couldn't remember seeing one in the cottage. 'Would you mind if we had the door open?' he said suddenly to Mrs Bryant, unable any longer to bear the torturing heat.

'It is a bit on the warm side,' Mrs Bryant agreed. She crossed to the door and flung it open; Kelsey threw the sergeant a look of unbounded gratitude.

'I came out of school with Miss Marshall,' Heather continued resolutely, 'and we walked along with Jill and Clive Egan.' She finally reached the point at which she could answer the Chief's question. 'I can't remember Miss Marshall saying anything about anyone calling at her cottage.'

No fresh inspiration about Ken Bryant had so far

struck the Chief during his ten minutes in the cottage. And it's not likely to strike me here, in this steam-bath, he thought sourly. He looked across at Bryant sitting apparently relaxed and at ease in the sauna-like atmosphere. I can't stand this much longer, the Chief thought—nor could be keep the Bryants any longer from their dinner. He glanced at Lambert and saw the sergeant's eyelids beginning to droop. He pushed back his chair and stood up.

As the two policemen went out into the dazzling glare of the afternoon a couple of minutes later Heather ran down the garden path in front of them and disappeared into the cottage next door. Kelsey drew in great lungfuls of air—warm, but nowhere near as warm as the air in the kitchen. 'A man like Bryant,' he said to Lambert as they walked back to the quarry run-in, 'out in the open air all day—how in heaven's name can he tolerate that infernal heat? And eat a cooked dinner on top of it?'

They reached the car and he sank into the passenger seat. 'A long cold drink,' he said with fervour. 'And pronto.' He closed his eyes and blew out a weary breath. 'Stop at the first place you see. As soon as we're clear of Longmead.'

CHAPTER 20

The inquest on Janet Marshall was a brief, formal affair, opened and adjourned, as was to be expected. There was the usual crowd of curious idlers and hopeful sensation-seekers. And several faces Kelsey recognized from Longmead village.

He felt a sour twinge of indigestion begin to twist his stomach as he made his way out of the Cannonbridge courthouse at the end of the proceedings. A little way ahead of him he caught sight of the silvery head and beaky profile of George Pickthorn. And not far behind Pickthorn, Mrs Bryant, dressed for the occasion in her most sober summer outfit, a two-piece Crimplene suit in broad chevron stripes that seemed to offer an echo of her cooking in their tones of cream and ginger, nutmeg and cinnamon.

She was chatting with animation to her Mayfield neighbour, Mrs Abell, nervous and unnoticeable as a shadow in a dark grey cotton dress and a small black hat unrelieved by any trimming. She looked like a pre-war newspaper photograph of a woman newly released from Holloway.

As Kelsey reached the exit he was approached by a couple of reporters. He began to shake his head as soon as he laid eyes on them. No comment, no statement, far too early.

It was comparatively easy to get rid of the man from the county journal, an old hand who knew the drill, but the evening paper had sent along a brash youngster who clearly fancied himself in the role of crime reporter. He wasn't to be dismissed without a struggle.

'Are you proposing to carry out a reconstruction of the crime?' he asked with a bright alert look. 'Dress up a policewoman and get her to walk along the lane to Rose Cottage?'

'I am not,' Kelsey said briefly. He wasn't addicted to fancy-dress gimmickry, he had never known a single piece of useful information come out of such capers.

The youngster persisted with three or four more questions of varying degrees of lunacy but Kelsey finally managed to send him about his business without losing his temper.

At the foot of the steps a tall thin man in a dark grey suit stood waiting; judging by his glance, waiting for Kelsey. Oh yes, Henry Lloyd, Kelsey thought after a moment's pondering, recognizing the headmaster from the school photographs. Lloyd saw his look of recognition and stepped forward.

'You're back then,' Kelsey said.

'Only temporarily, I fear.' Lloyd moved his head in resignation. 'I have to get back right away to Ribbenhall.' He nodded over at his station wagon on the other side of the road. 'I had to come over to pick up some things from Parkwood.'

'You haven't managed to settle your aunt in yet then?'

'I'm making progress,' Lloyd said. 'I've found a woman who seems very suitable but she can only come for an hour or two a day at present. In another week she'll be able to start properly.' He paused. 'It's a terrible business, this—' He shook his head and sighed. 'I was in there—' He jerked his head up at the courthouse. 'I couldn't take it in, none of it seemed real.' His face looked old and tired, full of heavy creases.

'I detest inquests,' Kelsey said. 'Never have been able to stomach them.' The indigestion surged up again and he put a hand to his chest, pressing down on the breastbone. 'Have you remembered anything? Anything more than you've already told us?'

Lloyd shook his head. 'But I did speak to my wife on the phone. She said she's never been inside Rose Cottage.' In any case, Kelsey thought, all the fingerprints were now accounted for.

'What about the funeral?' Lloyd asked. 'I must attend.'

'Some time next week, I imagine. It's up to the Schofields.'

Kelsey went off to his car. As he came in sight of it he saw George Pickthorn standing beside the vehicle, looking about with a bright, birdlike eye.

'I hope you don't mind me waiting for you like this,' he said as Kelsey came up. 'I was at the inquest, I saw you were busy talking afterwards so I thought I wouldn't bother you there.'

'Something you've remembered?' With long-practised skill Kelsey's right hand unwrapped a soda mint inside his pocket and transferred it to his mouth with smooth sleight of hand.

'You asked if I spoke to anyone that Friday after Miss Marshall went by to Rose Cottage at a quarter past four,' Pickthorn said. 'I've thought about it and I have remembered, I did speak to some people.'

'Yes?' Kelsey said without colour in his tone.

'I saw Mrs Lloyd turn in at the school gate at half past four. I didn't speak to her, I was too far away, but she saw me in the garden. I waved at her and Barry and they both waved back—'

'Barry?' Kelsey echoed.

'He's a little Mongol boy, Mrs Lloyd looks after him sometimes. Then I went inside and had my tea. I'd just finished and washed up when I remembered I had to ring the shop in Cannonbridge about the wood for the summerhouse. That would be about five o'clock. I had to speak to three different people before I got it sorted out, I must have been a good ten minutes on the phone.'

'Let me have the name of the shop,' Kelsey said. 'And who it was you spoke to.'

Pickthorn gave him the details. 'You check what I've told you,' he said with a jerk of his head. 'You'll find it's perfectly OK.'

And half an hour later Kelsey did have it checked and sure enough, it was perfectly OK.

Early on Saturday morning, well ahead of the shopping crowds, Sergeant Lambert pulled out of the station fore-court with Kelsey sitting beside him in the passenger seat. They were headed for Chalford Bay; the Colletts were expecting them.

A pleasant breeze was blowing as they reached the

coast road. They drove past a golf-course, sand dunes, a large old country house turned into a hotel. New bungalows were strung out along the approach road but the town itself seemed little changed from its heyday as a Victorian watering-place.

The resort had a somnolent, relaxed air. Kelsey began to feel sleepy as he glanced out at the seafront boarding-houses, the row of bathing-huts along the shore, the little pier with its elegant ironwork. 'I used to be taken to places like this on holiday when I was a child,' he said to Lambert. Some remnant of innocence seemed to cling about the streets, the strollers on the promenade.

The Colletts lived in an old terrace on the outskirts of town. The house was tall and narrow with plenty of space inside and a long rear garden, neatly cultivated. Stephen Collett was busying himself while waiting for them by carrying on with his wallpaper-stripping—layers of it, decades old—in one of the attic bedrooms.

Alison Collett opened the door to them. She was a tall slender young woman with a great deal of thick dark-blonde hair drawn back into a shining coil at the nape of her neck. Her skin was lightly and evenly tanned to a smooth honey colour; her eyes, a vivid, translucent sea-green, provided a startling note of contrast with the delicate monotone of her face and hair.

'I haven't been able to take it in properly,' she said as she led the way into the sitting-room. Tears trembled in her eyes. A little girl, two or three years old, came running in from the garden. She came to an abrupt halt when she saw the strangers, she turned and ran out again.

'Have you any idea—' Alison began but Kelsey interrupted her.

'We're only at a very early stage of the investigation. We're simply examining every possibility at present.'

There were running steps down the stairs and Stephen Collett came into the room, rolling down his sleeves. He was very tall and very fair, with a Scandinavian look, he could easily have been taken for Alison's brother. He introduced himself and went off to the kitchen to make coffee. Kelsey stood looking out at the garden, at the baby asleep in his pram in the dappled shade of a sycamore.

'Anything you can tell us that might be at all helpful,' he said when Stephen came back with the tray. 'Any special friends Janet had, any worries or problems, any plans, quarrels, broken engagements. Anything from the past, anything at all that might throw a glimmer of light.'

Alison handed round the coffee. 'We hadn't seen her since April,' she said. 'We spent a weekend with her at Ivydene when Lisa was on her honeymoon. She told us she'd fixed up about the job at Longmead and we drove her over there. She wanted us to take a look at Rose Cottage.

'I often stayed at Ivydene before I was married,' she added. 'When I was still living at home in Ellenborough.' After her marriage she and Stephen spent a weekend from time to time with her parents in Ellenborough and in the course of the weekend they would usually drive over to Ivydene for an afternoon or evening.

She had exchanged letters regularly with Janet but no, she hadn't kept any of the letters, it wasn't her custom. 'She seemed happy at Longmead,' she said. 'Judging from her letters. She liked the situation of the cottage, the privacy, she seemed to have settled in well.' She drank her coffee. 'She was happy at the school and she liked the headmaster.' He didn't interfere with her teaching in any way, he was helpful if she asked for help but otherwise he let her get on with it. She had never mentioned any problems or disagreements, there had been no trouble with any of the parents, or with anyone else in the village.

'What about men friends?' Kelsey asked.

'She didn't have any,' Alison said at once.

'You're very sure about that. Couldn't there have been someone you didn't know about?'

She hesitated, then she said, 'She had a block about men, she couldn't bear anything like that.' She clasped her hands. 'When she was a girl, a child really, nine or ten, when we were at school together, there was a man—' She pressed her hands tightly together. 'He molested her. She didn't tell anyone about it, she only told me some time afterwards and she made me promise not to tell anyone. Her father was very ill at the time, it wasn't long before his death. I think she felt it would be too much for her mother to cope with, on top of everything else. Mrs Marshall was a nice woman but a bit helpless.'

She turned her head and looked out of the window. 'It terrified and disgusted her. She told me once, years later, when we were at college, that she had nightmares about it for a long time, and even then, when she was grown up, the nightmares came back if she was tired or strained.' She drew a long, sighing breath. 'I think it got mixed up somehow with her father's illness and death, and all the worry at that time. Anyway, the result was that it put her off any sort of ordinary loving relationship with a man. People used to think she was cold and stand-offish but of course they didn't understand why she seemed like that.' She shook her head. 'I don't think she'd ever have changed, I could never see her getting married.'

'She always behaved quite normally with me,' Stephen said. 'And with any man in the ordinary way. She didn't freeze up when a man came into the room, or anything obvious like that, she behaved perfectly naturally. But if a man made any kind of advance to her, then he came smack up against a stone wall.'

'They used to call her the iceberg at college.' Alison put a hand up to her face. 'It wasn't that she wasn't accustomed to men.' She told Kelsey about the years in Ellenborough after the death of Janet's father, the lodgers, the long succession of businessmen.

Yes, she'd have learned an attitude to men in those twelve years, Kelsey thought, how to deal with them, always polite but never in the slightest degree encouraging. There must have been many an eye for her as she grew up into that arresting beauty, many an invitation and suggestion.

Stepphen poured more coffee. 'She seemed content to think of herself as a permanent spinster. She often used the expression about herself.'

'Did she seem frustrated or unhappy?'

'Not in the least. She liked teaching and she was fond of children. She made a great fuss of our two, she was godmother to the baby.' He paused. 'You couldn't say she was neurotic in any way. It was just as if something had been cut out of her life but what was left was wholesome and happy.'

Alison suddenly began to cry in a quiet, controlled way and Stephen crossed over to sit on the arm of her chair; he put a hand on her shoulder.

'Did she mention the people up at Mayfield Farm?' Kelsey asked. 'Do you know how she got on with them? If she had any dealings with them apart from renting the cottage and buying her milk there?'

'I don't think she had any other dealings,' Stephen said. 'She didn't say much about them, she gave the impression they were good landlords, that she didn't have any problems there.' He tilted his head back. 'She seemed to have a good opinion of the farmer's wife, I remember her saying she thought her very competent. She admired competence in women, she set great store by independence and self-sufficiency.' The opposite of her mother, Sergeant Lambert thought.

'There was a young workman from the farm,' Stephen recalled. 'When we took her over to look at Rose Cottage we walked across the fields and Janet spoke to him.'

'Neil Fleming?' Kelsey said.

'I don't remember his name. Sandy-haired chap, boyish-looking, a lot of freckles. He and Janet seemed on good terms, friendly and neighbourly, that sort of thing.'

'What's your opinion of the Schofields?' Kelsey asked.

Alison had stopped crying. 'I've known Lisa a lot longer than Derek,' she said in a voice that was under control again. 'Lisa's always been Janet's baby sister to me, I've pushed her out in her pram. Her mother spoiled her but Janet always fought against that—not with much success, I'm afraid. I'm sure that's why Janet left Ivydene, to give Lisa a chance to grow up.' She frowned. 'I don't really dislike Lisa but—'

'She can be a pain in the neck,' Stephen said. 'She expects everyone to dance attendance on her.' He grimaced. 'Mrs Marshall would have been horrified if she knew her little darling had actually married Schofield. She didn't think him anywhere near good enough.'

'I don't know that she would have married him if her mother was still alive,' Alison said. 'I think she half sees him as a substitute parent.' She looked reflectively at Kelsey. 'Some of those marriages turn out surprisingly well.'

'What was Schofield's attitude to Janet?' Kelsey asked.

She moved her shoulders. 'We didn't see them together all that often. My impression is that he had a rather placatory manner towards her.'

'He has a placatory manner towards everyone,' Stephen said.

She inclined her head. 'Ye . . . es, maybe—but particularly with Janet. I think he saw her as Lisa's guardian, the head of the family—after Mrs Marshall died.'

'And a much more formidable head of the family than Mrs Marshall,' Stephen added. 'Janet had twice the character of her mother.'

'Was he pleased when Janet moved out of Ivydene?'

Alison pondered the idea. 'I can't really say either way. At the time I took it for granted he'd be delighted, that he'd want to have the house to themselves, but I've no actual grounds for thinking that.'

'You told me just now,' Kelsey said in an expressionless tone, 'that Janet was digusted by any kind of approach from men. Did you ever get the impression that that could have been why she left Ivydene?'

CHAPTER 21

Alison looked startled. 'You mean, did Schofield make some sort of approach to her? And she wondered how he'd behave towards her after he moved in?'

'Or did Lisa get such an idea into her head,' Stephen put in. 'Start getting jealous fits, moody tantrums?'

Kelsey moved his shoulders. 'Something like that.'

Alison frowned. 'I can't ever remember getting such an impression.'

'It certainly never crossed my mind,' Stephen agreed. 'And Janet never hinted at anything like that. Schofield seemed besotted with Lisa, he scarcely took his eyes off her.'

'Do you know if Janet had anything specific against him? Apart from not considering him a suitable match for Lisa?'

'She never mentioned anything specific,' Alison said. 'She did say more than once that he wasn't very open or forthcoming.'

'Not that she would hold that against him in itself.' Stephen smiled slightly. 'There was no one who liked a larger area of privacy than Janet. But she didn't like him being so much older than Lisa and she did wonder about his life before they knew him.'

'Did she ever mention having enquiries made?' Kelsey asked. Sergeant Lambert was still looking into that; so far he'd come up with nothing.

Alison shook her head. 'No, never. I think she hoped right up to the day of the marriage that it wouldn't take place.' They both looked at Kelsey with unspoken questions: Was there something to find out? Is there something you know? Kelsey looked back at them, bland and neutral.

'Of course she could have made enquiries and drawn a blank,' Stephen said.

'That weekend you spent at Ivydene in April—do you recall any episode about a letter? Any letter arriving that seemed to disturb her?' They both shook their heads.

'Did she in any of her letters ever mention any admirers—even jokingly? Perhaps just a passing reference to some man that had made an approach that she'd rejected?' Again they shook their heads.

'I wouldn't expect her to,' Alison said. 'She never referred to anything like that.'

'Do you think Schofield felt she was against him? That she was hounding him?' Kelsey said in as light a tone as he could command. The word paranoid inserted itself into the air but no one spoke it.

Stephen considered the idea. 'It's possible, I suppose, but we don't really know him well enough to say.'

'The idea doesn't immediately strike you as ludicrous?'

Stephen shook his head slowly, in silence.

'Did she ever say anything about Schofield that puzzled you at the time? Some passing remark, perhaps, that she didn't enlarge on?'

'I can't recall anything.'

'If you do,' Kelsey said, 'or if you remember anything else, anything at all you think might be of use, get in touch.'

*

'They're a handsome family,' Kelsey observed to Lambert
as they set off on the return journey a little later. Lambert
murmured something in reply. He gazed out at the
candyfloss stalls, the toddlers staggering round on the
sand, the kites flying in the breeze, and imagined himself
coming home in the evenings to a tall slender young
woman with dark-blonde hair and sea-green eyes. It was a
full minute before his imagination supplied the other side
of the picture, the pram-pushing, night-time feeds,
endless washing, Saturday mornings spent stripping
paper from attic walls.

'We'll stop and get an ice-cream,' Kelsey said.

They picked their way between yelling youngsters,
cricketing fathers, donkey-rides, stalls with striped
awnings, selling a stunning variety of rock in every
conceivable shape, size and colour. Kelsey insisted on old-
fashioned cornets topped with thick yellow ice-cream, the
ice-cream of his childhood. They stood leaning against a
wooden groyne, eating them.

Nearby a lad sent a ball sailing through the air. The
Chief fielded it neatly and threw it back.

'That ball Heather Abell mentioned,' he said suddenly.
'The red and yellow ball belonging to the lad at the Mare
and Colt. Janet Marshall said she'd take it along there
and give it back to him.'

'There was certainly no red and yellow ball at Rose
Cottage,' Lambert said. 'I suppose the lad could have
remembered it, he could have run back and met Janet in
the lane, after she'd parted from the two girls. She could
have given him the ball then.'

'Possible.' Kelsey removed a dribble of ice-cream from
the side of the cornet with the tip of his tongue. 'Easy
enough to check.'

'Or she may not have taken the ball out of school. She
could have changed her mind and put it in a cupboard,

she had a lot to carry. She could have intended to pick it up later.'

'Could be.' Easy enough to check that too.

The Chief finished his cornet, managing to resist the temptation to sink totally back into unregenerate boyhood with potato crisps, peanut brittle and a thousand other delights. He took out a handkerchief and dabbed at his face and hands. 'Right then,' he said, refreshed, ready for anything. 'Back to Cannonbridge. Let's get cracking.'

CHAPTER 22

Janet Marshall's funeral was arranged for Wednesday afternoon at two-thirty. The vicar who held the joint livings of Stanbourne and Longmead was old now and ailing. He lived in the Stanbourne rectory and the services at Longmead were increasingly taken by a curate from one of the Cannonbridge churches. But the old man had known and liked Miss Marshall and he was determined to take the funeral service himself.

The afternoon was somewhat fresher and a welcome breeze rippled the tops of the churchyard trees. The little church was crowded with villagers from Longmead and Stanbourne, and there were a number of idlers and sightseers from Cannonbridge.

Shortly before the service began Kelsey took his place at the back of the church beside Sergeant Lambert and Constable Drew. The villagers were neat and sober in their dress, silent in their demeanour. The townspeople and sightseers were easy to pick out by their brighter clothes and the fact that they looked about with freedom and felt no inhibition about chatting to each other.

Jill and Heather were ranged with the other schoolchildren in pews at the front of the church. The Bryants were there, Mollie in a new black straw hat with a frivolous little veil and a suit the colour of a ripe aubergine, speckled with black dots like currants. Neil Fleming sat behind the Bryants, with the Slaters.

The Schofields and Colletts occupied a pew together, Lisa in dramatic black with a large hat draped with a veil. She held a lacy handkerchief to her eyes and her shoulders shook with suppressed sobs from the moment she entered the church, supported by her husband and Alison Collett.

Henry Lloyd sat next to Mrs Dunbar, the Stanbourne headmistress; he looked neither to left nor right but stared fixedly ahead. In the pew behind them George Pickthorn's silvery head bobbed from left to right as he darted his gaze over the congregation.

There were so many wreaths and sheaves, bunches of garden flowers, posies from the children, that in spite of everything the church could hardly escape something of a festive air. Where Kelsey sat, the scent of flowers mingled uneasily with a penetrating odour of mothballs released from the dark funeral suits of ruddy-faced farmers and their full-fleshed wives, sitting in nearby pews.

The service began. The vicar was assisted by one of the Cannonbridge curates, in case he found himself unable to continue, but he bore up well and didn't have to retire.

Outside in the churchyard sunlight glittered the leaves and birds sang sweetly as the committal took place. Most of the schoolchildren were crying now. Mrs Bryant wiped her eyes and Lisa Schofield stood with her head buried against her husband's shoulder.

'I don't see young Egan,' Kelsey murmured to Constable Drew.

'His landlady's here,' Drew said. 'Mrs Turnbull.' He nodded over at her and Kelsey followed his gaze. He saw a spry little woman in her sixties with a sharp face and a

keen, observant eye. She was standing beside Mrs
Abell—again in her released-prisoner outfit of dark grey
cotton dress and small black hat—and old Mrs Perrin,
Mrs Abell's mother, standing solid and unshakable with
her stout black shoes planted squarely down eighteen
inches apart on the baked earth. She wore a heavy old-
fashioned black coat shiny with age, and a black felt hat
that had seen a great many funerals. Mrs Abell was
dabbing furtively at her eyes but Mrs Perrin looked
philosophically about, having outlived tears.

When it was all over and they were walking to the car
parked a little way along the road, Constable Drew
glanced over at the Slaters and Neil Fleming setting off
together to walk back to the farm.

'I was in the Greyhound at Stanbourne last night,' he
told the Chief. 'I heard a bit of news that might interest
you. Young Fleming's looking for another job.'

Kelsey came to an abrupt halt.

'A farmer I know over at Broadwood,' Drew went on.
Broadwood was a hamlet some ten miles away. 'He's been
advertising for a stockman for the last few weeks. I asked
him if he was having any luck. He said he'd had one or
two promising replies, one the other day from young
Fleming at Mayfield.'

After Drew had gone off to his own vehicle Kelsey stood
frowning fiercely down at the parched grass. Oswald
Slater had told him he was well satisfied with Fleming, he
expected him to stay four or five years.

'I've had the feeling all along,' Kelsey said to Sergeant
Lambert, 'that the answer's up there at the farm.' He
struck his fists together. 'I'm damned certain one or more
of them's not telling the whole truth.'

'I suppose it couldn't have been one of the two
farmworkers who killed her?' Lambert said. 'And the
other one's shielding him?'

Kelsey performed some elaborate facial gestures,

considering the idea. 'They knew Slater was out and wouldn't be back for some time. They could have started larking about and got into a silly mood. They see Miss Marshall just after she gets home from school, perhaps she steps outside the back door for a moment. One of them goes up to the back door, just a stupid prank, going to try his luck with her, see if he can melt the iceberg, he may have a bet on with his mate.'

He stared up at the sky, streaked with gauzy ribbons of cloud. 'He gets inside the cottage on some pretext, he gets more than he bargained for. She has this fierce reaction, she starts to scream. He tries to stop her, he loses his head, pulls the scarf round her neck. Then he runs back panic-stricken and tells his mate what's happened, throws himself on his mercy: You'll say I was here working with you all the time—they'll think it was some stranger breaking in.'

'Fleming's only been at Mayfield six months or so,' Lambert pointed out. Scarcely long enough to form a bond between the two men strong enough to make one of them risk that kind of involvement in order to shield the other. 'I suppose it's not possible they were both in it together?'

'You mean they both went to the cottage?' Kelsey bit his top lip. 'I can't see that.'

Lambert moved his head. 'No, I suppose not.'

They reached the car. 'We'll go up to Mayfield,' Kelsey said. They got in and Lambert drove to the farm in thoughtful silence.

The Slaters and Neil Fleming were in the big kitchen, talking over the funeral service. Ken Bryant had gone home to change his clothes and have a bite to eat before returning to work. Mrs Slater, still in her dark suit and little cloche hat, offered to make tea but Kelsey refused. She reminds me of someone, dressed like that, he thought, but the recollection eluded him.

'If we could have a word with Neil,' he said to Slater. 'One or two details I'd like to check.'

'Yes, of course.' Slater took the three of them across the hall to the sitting-room, he went out and closed the door behind him. Fleming didn't sit down but stood looking at the two policemen with a closed, wary face.

Kelsey walked over to the window and opened it wide. He took his time about selecting a chair, sitting down, making himself comfortable. Fleming leaned back against the sideboard with his elbow resting on the polished surface. All the lines of his body expressed tension.

'Why are you leaving here?' Kelsey asked suddenly.

Fleming looked down at the floor, then he raised his head. 'I fancy a change.'

'When you came here six months ago you told Slater you intended staying a few years.'

'I'm not learning as much as I expected.' Fleming's manner was uneasy, tinged with defiance. 'And it's too quiet here, I like a bit more life.'

'You fancy there'll be more life over at Broadwood? You think you'll learn more on a farm half the size of Mayfield?'

Fleming made no reply but closed his eyes with a mutinous look.

'No other reason?' Kelsey persisted. Fleming shook his head slowly and stubbornly. He's lying, Kelsey thought, the air's full of it. 'Where were you between four-thirty and five-thirty that Friday afternoon?' he asked abruptly.

'I've already told you,' Fleming said on a note of anger. 'I was working with Ken Bryant on the fencing.'

'You didn't go down to the back door of Rose Cottage? To pay Miss Marshall a visit?'

Fleming shook his head with silent force.

'Did you go inside the cottage at all that afternoon? For any reason? Alone or with Bryant?' Again Fleming shook his head.

Kelsey rose suddenly to his feet and Fleming glanced at him in surprise. The Chief said nothing further, he didn't look at Fleming but left the room and went briskly back into the kitchen, followed by Lambert. 'There's nothing more for the moment,' he told Mrs Slater with an affable air.

He and Lambert went out into the sun-drenched afternoon. Kelsey paused by the car and stood looking across at the new fencing, solid and substantial. 'Drive round to the quarry run-in,' he said abruptly to Lambert. 'We'll leave the car there and walk round to Bryant's place.'

Ken was sitting eating at the kitchen table, dressed now in his working clothes. Mrs Bryant, still in her speckled funeral suit but with her hat removed, was drinking tea, pondering with mournful brooding the conduct of the funeral.

'Did you want to speak to the girls?' she asked Kelsey. 'I'm afraid they're not here.' They'd gone back to a schoolfriend's house after the service, they wouldn't be home for another hour.

'No, it's not the girls I want to talk to,' Kelsey said. 'I'd like a word with your husband.' He refused Mrs Bryant's offer to make them fresh tea.

Ken drained his cup and got to his feet. 'I can't stop long,' he said. 'I must get back to work.'

'We won't delay you, we'll walk back up the field with you.' This suited the Chief very well. He had no wish to question Ken in front of his wife, he would be far more likely to keep his mouth close-buttoned in Mollie's presence.

'Right you are then,' Ken said amicably. They left the house and walked down the garden to the wicket gate. The flower borders were full of sweet william, Canterbury bells, Virginia stocks, the rockery tumbled over with flame-coloured nasturtiums. Kelsey made some casual observation about the funeral. As soon as they were through the gate, out of sight of the house, he halted.

'Would you be prepared,' he said without preamble, 'to go into court and swear that you and Fleming were working together on the fencing all that Friday afternoon?'

Ken gave him a startled look. 'Yes, of course I would,' he said after a moment.

'And in particular, between half past four and half past five?'

There was another brief pause before Ken said, 'Yes.'

There was again a little silence, then Kelsey said, 'Why is Fleming looking for another job?'

Ken looked thunderstruck. 'That's news to me.'

'He hasn't mentioned it to you?'

'He certainly has not.'

'Can you think of any reason why he should suddenly decide to leave?' Ken made no reply but stood looking down at the grass.

'Could it be,' Kelsey said harshly, 'because he's responsible for the death of Janet Marshall?'

Bryant uttered a sound of surprised disclaimer.

'You'd have had to know about it of course,' Kelsey said. 'You'd have had to cover up for him.'

'That's a load of rubbish,' Bryant said with heat. 'He was nowhere near the cottage, he was—' He broke off.

In the distance Kelsey saw Mrs Slater—changed now from her suit into working clothes—cross the field and walk over to where the goats grazed behind the fence. Something clicked in his brain. He remembered all at once who it was she reminded him of—a woman years ago, when he was a young constable, the wife of a sergeant; one of the inspectors got involved with her. In the end the inspector was transferred and it all blew over. The woman's face rose up at him now, an ordinary-looking woman but with something of the same air as Margaret Slater, the same look in the eyes.

'Fleming was up at the house,' he said softly. 'With Mrs Slater.' And knew by the jerk of Bryant's head that he was right.

CHAPTER 23

'How long was Fleming up at the house?' Kelsey asked.

Bryant stood for a moment in silence, looking down at the ground, then he said, 'From half past four till half past five.'

'So we come back,' Kelsey said in the same soft tone, 'to the question: Why is Fleming looking for another job? Perhaps he's done a bit of thinking. He knows he was up at the house and he knows you were alone down here in the field. He's come to the conclusion it could have been you that killed Janet Marshall. He intends to be clear of Mayfield before it all comes out — and Slater learns what's been going on with his wife.'

Bryant took a step backwards 'You can't possibly believe —'

'Oh, it's perfectly possible,' Kelsey said. 'The fencing was a two-handed job, you couldn't carry on for long by yourself. Did you start to think: Neil's up at the house amusing himself, I think I'll go down to Rose Cottage and try my luck there. A good-looking young woman, right on your doorstep, I dare say you'd often fancied her.'

'I'm a married man,' Bryant said with protest. A nerve jumped sharply beside his eye.

'Easy enough to get yourself admitted on some pretext,' Kelsey said. 'But things don't go as planned. She's terrified, disgusted, she begins to shout, she won't be quietened. Was it your hands that grabbed her scarf? Pulled it tight round her throat?'

Bryant dropped his head into his hands. 'Why would I

do a terrible thing like that?'

'Why would anyone do it?'

Bryant raised his head. 'I was nowhere near the cottage.' His voice was firm again, louder. 'I was up at the turkey sheds. I went up there when Neil went up to the house. I put in an hour or so and then when Neil came out of the house again I went back down with him and we carried on with the fencing.' He flung out a hand. 'I swear it.'

'Five minutes ago you were ready to swear you worked all afternoon on the fencing with Fleming.' Bryant stared up at the Chief without speaking.

Sergeant Lambert looked at Bryant, pale now and sweating; he wondered if Kelsey was going to take him in. But the Chief suddenly said, 'Did you mention to anyone else what was going on between Fleming and Mrs Slater?'

Bryant shook his head.

'Anyone at all?' Kelsey persisted. 'Your wife, for instance? Some mate at the pub?'

'I did not.' Bryant looked fiercely at the Chief. 'I'm no gossip. What people choose to get up to is their business, it's no concern of mine. I certainly don't go round the village chattering about it — the less I know about such things the better.'

Kelsey looked at him for some moments, then he said abruptly, 'Better get back to your job.' Bryant set off at once up the field at a rapid pace.

Kelsey stood looking after him, frowning, rubbing a finger along the side of his neck. 'We'll have to speak to Fleming and Mrs Slater,' he said to Lambert. They followed in the same direction as Bryant but more slowly; Bryant didn't turn round.

Kelsey walked in silence, pursing his lips, frowning fiercely. As they came to the top of the field Lambert looked across and saw Mrs Slater standing by the goats, adjusting a tether. She glanced over at the sound of their approach, she stood watching them as they came up to her.

Kelsey couldn't think of any delicate way of framing his question so he put it to her direct. 'I don't enjoy asking you this, but I can't avoid it. Did you spend an hour in the house that Friday afternoon with Neil Fleming?'

She stood stroking the silky white neck of the goat which went on placidly chewing. Then she said, 'Yes.' That was all. She asked no questions, made no appeal.

'You know Fleming's applied for another job?' Kelsey said.

She gave him a quick, surprised glance. However could I have thought her ordinary? he wondered, looking into the depths of those curious gold-flecked eyes. 'No, I didn't know,' she said. The look on her face added: But it explains a lot.

'It's over then,' Kelsey said to Lambert as they went back across the field. 'All Fleming wants to do now is get the hell out.'

A moment later they saw Fleming come out of one of the farm buildings. He saw them approach, and the direction from which they came.

Kelsey raised a hand and Fleming halted. When they came up to him the Chief said in a formal tone, 'I will put to you now the question I have just put to Mrs Slater, and which she has answered.' Fleming's jaw tightened. 'Were you in the house with Mrs Slater for an hour that Friday afternoon?'

Fleming gave a single nod.

'Between four-thirty and five-thirty?' Again Fleming nodded.

To Lambert's surprise the Chief said nothing more but strode off in the direction of the top road and the car.

'That lad Clive Egan,' he said as they walked along in the oppressive heat, 'he's some sort of relative of Ken Bryant—or Mrs Bryant. Suppose he saw something that

afternoon, some action of Ken's that he chanced to spot
and thought nothing of at the time, but remembered
later, after the body was found. He might very well decide
that the best thing he could do would be to forget all
about it.'

'Egan parted company with the two girls around half
past four,' Lambert said. That part of the timing was a
little vague, neither Egan nor the girls could say exactly
how long they had stood talking, they guessed five or ten
minutes. 'He could have seen or heard something as he
walked past Rose Cottage.'

Kelsey took out a handkerchief and dabbed at his
forehead. 'Say he caught sight of Ken Bryant for a
moment. Or heard Janet Marshall talking to someone at
her back door, heard her address Bryant by name, or
maybe he recognized Bryant's voice. If he mentioned it
later to Bryant, after the body was found, Bryant would
say: For God's sake don't go round saying that, you'll have
me in the dock. It definitely wasn't me you saw—or
heard, I was nowhere near the cottage. I was with
Fleming all that afternoon, working on the fencing, I can
prove I was, Fleming will swear I was.

'Egan could still have his doubts but he'd think: I
suppose I could be mistaken. And in any case, whatever
Ken Bryant was doing there at that time, he certainly
wasn't murdering Miss Marshall, he couldn't have had
anything to do with a terrible crime like that, not good
old Ken Bryant that I've known since I was a kid.' He
pressed his fingers into his cheek. 'We'll have another
word with Egan tomorrow, catch him when he gets in
from work.'

No. 4 Prospect Place was the end cottage of a row of four
near Stanbourne church. Clive Egan had just got home
from work when the police car pulled up. He was inside
the gate, turning round to close it, when he saw the car

approach. His eyes met Kelsey's and a look of fear, naked
and unmistakable, crossed his face. He flinched as if
someone were about to strike him.

The car went past him and halted. By the time the
Chief stepped out on to the pavement and came towards
him, Clive's look held nothing more than ordinary civil
enquiry. He stood waiting for them to come up.

'We won't keep you long,' the Chief said with brisk
affability. 'I expect you're ready for your tea.' Clive said
nothing, made no move. 'All right if we come inside?'
Kelsey said. 'I'd just as soon not conduct my business in
the street.'

'Yes, of course.' Clive didn't look at them, he opened
the gate and stood waiting for them to pass through. At
the downstairs front window Lambert saw the shadowy
figure of Egan's landlady behind the filmy curtains.

Clive opened the front door and stood back for them to
enter. The pungent, earthy odour of boiling beetroot
greeted them as they stepped across the threshold. The
door of the sitting-room opened a little way along the hall
and Mrs Turnbull came out, with a look of lively curiosity
on her sharp features.

'We're just going up to Clive's room to have a word with
him,' Kelsey told her in a tone of cheerful reassurance.
'Nothing to concern yourself about, we won't keep him
long.'

Clive led them up the narrow stairs to the second of two
bedrooms. The room was small, adequately furnished.
Two sets of overflowing bookshelves stood against the
walls, paperbacks were stacked on the floor. On a table
by the window a record-player stood beside a large pile of
records. Ranged along the mantelpiece and a set of wall
shelves were models of boats, cars, birds, in various
materials.

Kelsey picked up a model of a railway engine, surprisingly heavy, carved from wood, beautifully made with

loving detail, polished to a rich gleam. 'Do you do a lot of this kind of work?' he asked.

Clive nodded. Kelsey glanced about the cramped room. 'I do it down in the shed,' Clive said. 'In the back garden. Mrs Turnbull lets me have the shed to myself—I keep the garden tidy for her.'

'Sit down, lad.' Kelsey put the engine back on the shelf. 'No need to get alarmed, just a couple of points I'd like to go over.' He stood looking down at Clive. 'I want you to carry your mind back to that Friday afternoon when you walked along Mayfield Lane with Miss Marshall.' Clive's face closed and his features took on a look of stubborn wariness.

'After you left the girls you walked past Rose Cottage,' Kelsey said. Clive nodded. 'Did you glance in at all? At the cottage or the garden? Did you see or hear any-thing—or anyone? Someone local perhaps, someone you wouldn't be surprised to see there, someone you might think, looking back on it afterwards, after the discovery of the body: I expect he had a good reason to be there, I don't see any need to mention it to anyone, that would only cause unnecessary aggro, he couldn't possibly have had anything to do with the murder, he's not that sort of person.'

Clive shook his head. 'I didn't glance in.'

'You didn't see or hear anyone? Anyone at all?'

'No.'

'You're quite certain?'

'Yes.'

'The Bryants,' Kelsey said with one of his sudden changes of tack, 'they're relatives of yours?'

Clive looked surprised. 'Yes,' he said after a moment. 'My mother was a cousin of Mrs Bryant—I call her Aunt Mollie, I've always called her that. She and Uncle Ken knew my father too, they were all young together.'

'They've been good to you, the Bryants? You think a lot of them?'

'Yes, of course.' Clive's attitude remained tense. Sergeant Lambert had a strong impression of a restricted life, dammed-up energy, a personality shut in on itself.

Outside the door there was a whisper of sound. Kelsey rose silently and crossed the room; he flung the door suddenly open. Mrs Turnbull straightened up on the threshold and gave him a bright smile.

'I wondered if you'd like a cup of tea,' she said, totally unabashed.

'That's very kind of you. Yes, thank you, we would like some,' Kelsey said. 'Clive's just going to take us down to the shed to have a look at his models. We'll have the tea down there if that's all right with you. Clive can fetch it when it's ready.'

Mrs Turnbull went off down to the kitchen and Kelsey and Lambert followed her with Clive sandwiched between them. In the kitchen, steamy and odorous from the pan of beetroot boiling on the stove, Mrs Turnbull opened the back door and indicated a green shed, fairly large, stoutly built, standing some yards from the house. They stepped out into the warm evening air and walked down a neat cinder path between ranks of gooseberry bushes, raspberry canes, rows of lettuce and radishes, a strawberry patch, beds of old-fashioned cabbage roses.

The interior of the shed displayed the same pattern as Clive's bedroom, a great deal of material and work in progress, all arranged with reasonable neatness, no sign of obsessive tidiness. Large model planes hung from the ceiling; houses, churches, ships, animals, were ranged on shelves. A half-finished farm wagon, carved from wood, stood on a worktable.

Kelsey picked it up. 'Is this what you're doing at present?' he asked. Clive nodded but didn't relax his manner. He kept his shoulders hunched and his arms close to his sides. Kelsey wandered about, picking things up, putting them down, examining them, asking questions about tools and methods.

'Do you ever think of going in for carpentry?' he asked. 'You'd obviously be good at it.'

'I prefer general maintenance work.' Clive stood tense and rigid. 'You get out into the open air, I don't like being shut in.'

'Better go and collect the tea,' Kelsey said after a few minutes. As soon as Clive had left the shed the Chief walked swiftly round the interior, stooping, peering, moving, lifting, looking behind things. In one corner was an old pine cupboard; he opened the door and glanced inside. A row of woodworking tools was held in the slots of a rack fastened to the inside of the door. The cupboard shelves were filled with boxes, tins of lacquer, tubes of adhesive. The Chief leaned down and uttered a sudden exclamation.

On the bottom shelf, tucked in behind a pile of model-making magazines, was a red and yellow ball.

CHAPTER 24

Kelsey straightened up. Lambert glanced into the cupboard, following the Chief's gaze.

'I knew it,' Lambert said. 'I knew all along it was him.' Kelsey looked at him without speaking, an abstracted glance full of racing thought. He stood rubbing a finger along his chin.

There was a rattling sound outside and Clive came back down the garden carrying a tray. Kelsey closed the cupboard and remained standing beside it. Clive came into the shed and set down the tray, he began to pour out the tea. Kelsey took his cup and drank slowly, in silence.

Lambert ate a slice of fruit cake.

Kelsey suddenly spoke to Clive. 'Did you go inside the gate of Rose Cottage that afternoon for any reason at all? Some perfectly innocent reason?' Clive glanced up at him and shook his head.

'Did you perhaps take a harmless fancy to Miss Marshall?' Kelsey persisted. 'Perhaps you had a fancy for her when she was over at Stanbourne. Maybe you just wanted to talk to her?'

A slow flush rose in Clive's cheeks. 'I told you,' he said on a weary, stubborn note. 'I didn't go near the cottage.' He made no attempt to drink his tea.

'Then how do you account for that?' Kelsey suddenly reached across and threw open the cupboard door.

'For what?' Clive asked blankly.

Kelsey gestured down at the bottom shelf. 'For that ball.'

'Ball?' Clive echoed on a baffled note.

Kelsey stooped and pulled out the magazines. 'There,' he said. 'That ball.'

'Oh, that—I'd forgotten all about it.'

'How did you come by it?'

'I found it in the lane.'

'What lane?'

'Mayfield Lane. I picked it up.'

'Why?'

'I just saw it lying there. I thought: Some kid's lost that, might come looking for it.'

'When was this?'

Clive hesitated and his expression grew even more uneasy. 'It was that Friday,' he said at last. 'When I came home, when I came down here, I just chucked the ball into the cupboard. I meant to give it to Jill Bryant but I forgot. I never gave it another thought.'

'Where exactly did you pick it up? Outside Rose Cottage?'

'A little bit further on, at the side of the lane, in the long grass.'

'Among the things Miss Marshall was carrying home that day,' Kelsey said in a flat, neutral tone, 'was a red and yellow ball. There's no such ball now in Rose Cottage.' Nor in the school. Nor had the ball been returned to Stuart Hitchman. 'If that's the same ball—and it certainly looks to me as if it might be—then how do you account for its being where you found it?'

'She must have dropped it,' Clive said. 'She was carrying a lot of stuff.' He moved his head uneasily under Kelsey's gaze, he turned it suddenly away, like a dog. 'She'd have to put her bags down to open the gate, the ball could have rolled out then.'

'You didn't go to her funeral,' Kelsey said abruptly.

Clive blinked at the sudden switch. 'No,' he said after a moment.

'Your landlady went. Did she ask you to go with her?'

'Yes.'

'Why didn't you go?'

'I had to be at work.'

'You could have got time off.'

'I don't like funerals,' Clive said stubbornly. 'I can't see the good of all that fuss.'

'You saw the ball in the lane,' Kelsey said with another swift change of tack. 'You recognized it as one you had seen among the things Miss Marshall was carrying. You picked it up and went up to the door of Rose Cottage to return it.'

'I never went near the cottage,' Clive said with fierce protest. 'I keep telling you. I didn't know she had the ball—I never saw it among her things.'

Kelsey swallowed the last of his tea and set the cup down on the tray.

'You got as far as the front door. Then you lost your nerve and went off again. But while you were standing there you saw or heard something—or someone—inside the cottage. Someone you knew.'

Clive stood with his hands dug into his sides, his fists tight clenched. 'I told you,' he said again, 'I never went there.'

Kelsey reached into the cupboard and picked up the ball. 'I'll take this,' he said. 'If you should change your mind, if you want to tell me you did go to the cottage, you do know something, get in touch.'

He strode out of the shed, followed by Lambert. They didn't go back through the house but down the garden to a gate that led out on to a narrow lane. They walked along the lane and round the end of the terrace, back towards where they'd left the car.

'I thought for sure you were going to take him in,' Lambert said with a strong question in his voice. Kelsey jerked his shoulders but said nothing, he strode along with a set face.

'You've never really considered him,' Lambert said. 'I can't understand why not.' Still Kelsey made no reply. 'He was on the spot,' Lambert persisted. 'He had three-quarters of an hour to do it in. He came tearing up the lane red in the face and only just managed to catch the bus.'

Kelsey gave a long sigh as if being forced to speak at the point of a dagger. 'He's no murderer,' he said with finality, rationing Lambert to just that, no enlargement, no explanation.

'You can't possibly know that,' Lambert objected.

'I do know it.' The Chief hunched his shoulders and thrust his jaw stubbornly out.

But you can never just know, Lambert thought, reduced now to silent arguing inside his head. You can't possibly be sure.

'What is it makes you so certain?' he said aloud.

'I can't put it into words,' the Chief said on a warning

note of exasperation. 'But I'd take my oath on it.'

Lambert relapsed into silence and they reached the car. As Lambert got into the driver's seat and started the engine he glanced up at the house and saw Mrs Turnbull peering out without subterfuge from her front window, the curtains held boldly to one side. Her sharp features wore the astonished and baffled look of a polecat balked of its prey.

On Friday Chief Inspector Kelsey had to go over to Hayford. An embezzlement case, one in which he had taken a special interest, was coming up at the Crown Court.

He wasn't displeased at the interruption. It would be a relief to be able to forget Longmead for a few hours, let his subconscious get busy on the case in the interval, make what it could of the mass of facts and details. The Chief regarded his subconscious as a parent might regard a brilliant, sensitive child, never to be alarmed or directly interrogated, no oppressive demands ever to be made— just steal off quietly, give the little chap his head and see what he's come up with, clever little fellow, by the time you get back.

And in any case Friday was a good day to be away from Longmead. The village hall had to be cleared out and handed back in good order on Friday afternoon. A twenty-first birthday party was due to be held there on Saturday evening; the booking was of long standing.

It was Saturday afternoon before the Chief got over to Longmead again. 'We'd better look in at the hall,' he told Sergeant Lambert. 'Just to see everything's in order.' Everything was in order and they went along afterwards to Rose Cottage.

Dusty sunlight slanted in at the windows as the Chief wandered through the rooms, hoping for some fresh burst of inspiration. The cottage had an air of suspension as if waiting for someone to step back inside and begin the process of living in it again. 'It'll be long enough before Slater finds anyone to rent it,' Kelsey said as he prowled round. Folk were notoriously reluctant to live in a place that had been the scene of a violent crime.

They went out into the garden, already beginning to look overgrown and neglected. In the vegetable plot bolted lettuce reared yellowing misshapen heads beside a row of fine scarlet runners heavy with long straight bunches that would never now be picked. Kelsey felt all at once tired and stale, sick of it all. Sunday tomorrow, he'd get his head down, have a good long sleep, let it all stew till Monday.

From the garden next door came the sound of a motorbike revving—Dave Bryant no doubt, cherishing his machine. Dave was one of the few males in the neighbourhood who could be absolutely ruled out. They'd checked at the college and he definitely had been there all that Friday, from half-past eight in the morning, no shred of doubt. The party had lasted until close on midnight and Dave had been active and visible to the end.

The voices of Jill and Heather floated across, shrill and teasing, the sound of their running, peals of laughter. Ken Bryant called to the girls from the back door of his cottage, asking if they'd seen his secateurs. An ordinary Saturday afternoon, peaceful domestic occupations. Kelsey felt sour and isolated, a perpetual outsider on the fringes of other lives.

'Come on,' he said abruptly to Lambert. 'Back to Cannonbridge.' See what was doing, get a bite to eat, with luck get off early for once.

They walked back to the quarry run-in, past Mollie Bryant dozing on her porch, old Mrs Perrin assiduously knitting and rocking, George Pickthorn perched on a ladder at the far end of his garden, picking plums and waving away wasps. The village was settling back into everyday existence, it had swallowed the crime, was beginning to digest it.

They reached the car. Kelsey got in and settled himself back against the upholstery. Sleepiness began to steal over him but he resisted the temptation to close his eyes.

As they drove up a long rise he saw in the distance an old blue station wagon parked on the grass verge by the church. 'That's Lloyd's car,' he said. 'He must be back.' He couldn't be bothered with the headmaster now, Monday would be soon enough.

Two women got out of the vehicle and went round to the rear. They opened the doors and began taking out containers of flowers, setting them down on the grass. One of the women picked up a couple of baskets of blooms and went off with them up to the church. Kelsey recognized her slight figure, her rapid scuttling walk.

'That's Mrs Abell,' he said to Lambert. 'I imagine the other one's Mrs Lloyd.' The second woman turned at the sound of their car and gave them a sharp glance. Taller and heavier than Mrs Abell, dressed in a beige skirt and cardigan, a crisp white blouse; nothing of the scuttler or scurryer about her. She stepped out into the road and raised a commanding hand.

'We'll have to stop,' Kelsey said with a long sigh. He rearranged his features into a look of amiability.

'I'm Rachel Lloyd,' the woman said as they got out of the car. She smiled and held out her hand. 'You must be Chief Inspector Kelsey.' In the bright afternoon light her face looked fresh and vigorous, almost handsome.

'I've only just got back,' she said. 'I made sure I was back in time to do the flowers, it's my turn on the roster.' She barely paused for breath. 'What a dreadful business, poor Miss Marshall, I could scarcely credit it. It was a terrible shock for poor Henry.' Mercifully she didn't appear to require the Chief to take any part in the exchange—other than to stand docilely by and listen.

She resumed her task of removing the flowers from the station wagon. Her voice flowed relentlessly on, about the murder, its effect on the village, her opinions about it all. Kelsey felt hypnotized by the sound.

Mrs Abell came scurrying back down the path and picked up a metal container of foliage. She gave the two men a nod and a sidelong glance as she darted off again.

'She cleans the brasses while I do the vases,' Mrs Lloyd said. 'She's very thorough, quite invaluable.' She set down a jug of early chrysanthemums, yellow and bronze, a trug full of spiky dahlias, richly amber. 'I could see no point in my coming back for the funeral, I told Henry so over the phone and he quite agreed with me. In my opinion there's been far too much morbid excitement in the village over this unfortunate affair.'

A hairpin became dislodged from the thick knot of chestnut hair, streaked with grey, at the nape of her neck. She retrieved the pin and stabbed it home. 'And I can't say that I approve of the way the schoolchildren were allowed to attend the funeral *en masse* like that. It can't have been at all healthy for young minds.'

Kelsey nerved himself to interrupt the flow. If he didn't get food and rest soon he would either fall fast asleep on his feet or keel over from hunger.

'If you and your husband would call in at the station on Monday—' he began but she broke in.

'Yes, of course, we intend doing that.' She swept resolutely on. 'Janet Marshall didn't really enter into village life, such a pity. When she first came here I did my best to interest her in one or two of my little projects but I soon saw I was wasting my time. There's so much one can do in a village like this, helping with the old folk, one or two mentally handicapped people, a little Mongol child—'

'Oh yes.' Kelsey remembered George Pickthorn

mentioning the child.

'Barry Finch,' Mrs Lloyd said. 'The mother's a high-grade mental defective. Barry's a friendly, good-natured little chap.'

'You had him with you in the car that Friday afternoon when you called at the school?' Kelsey said with a surreptitious glance at his watch.

'Did I?' She frowned, casting her mind back. 'Oh yes, I believe I did. I had intended to run Barry home first but I was a bit on the late side so I took him along with me to the school to explain to Henry, then I ran Barry home.'

The Chief's stomach uttered a loud warning growl.

'Henry didn't mind,' Mrs Lloyd said. 'The last day of term, he could find plenty of little jobs to do.'

Kelsey frowned. 'You mean your husband didn't go with you in the car when you ran Barry home?'

'No, of course not, there would have been no point in that. Barry lives out at Prior's Hill, that's in the opposite direction from Parkwood. And in any case, I had to go back to the school again, to pick up the exhibition stuff. I couldn't stop to take it then, I couldn't keep Mrs Finch waiting any longer. She gets so anxious over any little trifle, she'd begin to imagine all sorts of disasters had happened to Barry.'

'What time did you get back to the school — after you ran the child home?'

She considered. 'I suppose it would be about ten past, a quarter past five.'

Kelsey exchanged a glance with Lambert. Bang goes Ken Bryant as our man, the look said. Bryant couldn't have crossed the field and slipped down to the back door of Rose Cottage unobserved. He was working only a few yards away from the window of the headmaster's office. And Lloyd was still there, was there right up until a quarter past five, he would have seen him.

CHAPTER 25

Mrs Lloyd reached into the station wagon and took out a basket of mauve asters. 'Henry said he had a cupboard to clear out in his classroom, so he didn't mind having to wait.'

'In his classroom?' Kelsey echoed. 'He didn't stay in his office while you were gone? What exactly did he do? Please try to be precise. We're trying to build up an accurate picture of everything that happened that afternoon, every detail is important.'

'Yes, I understand.' She tilted back her head and closed her eyes. 'I told Henry about running Barry home and he said: That's all right, I can clear out the cupboard. He closed up in the office and shut the window, then he came out and closed the door. He walked with me to his classroom while we were talking and he was still in his classroom when I got back.'

Kelsey exchanged another glance with Lambert: So it could have been Bryant after all. Lloyd's classroom didn't overlook the field or the rear approach to Rose Cottage. If Bryant saw Lloyd close the office window, heard the station wagon drive off again, he'd conclude it was all clear there, the school was now empty.

'You're absolutely certain about this?' the Chief persisted.

'Yes, absolutely. But why don't you go along and ask Henry about it if it's so important? He'll confirm what I've just told you. He's at home now, he got back from Ribbenhall this morning. He managed to fix my aunt up with a suitable woman. He's been very good, very patient about it all. You'll find him out in the garden, I left him starting work there, everything's shot up so while we've both been away.'

Mrs Abell came hurrying back again and picked up a jug of fern. 'I don't seem to have brought any gypsophila,' Mrs Lloyd said suddenly. 'I was sure I'd put some in. I know I cut plenty.'

Lloyd was down by the shrubbery at the far end of the garden; they could hear the sound of his shears as they got out of the car. The garden had indeed begun to run riot; loosestrife and campanula, blue flax and veronica spilled exuberantly out over the borders.

The headmaster didn't hear them coming, the rhythmic clipping of his shears deadened the swish of their footsteps in the long grass. He paused and stepped back to assess his efforts, he took out a handkerchief and wiped his brow. As he put the handkerchief back in his pocket he turned and caught sight of them.

'Hello there!' he called out. 'I was coming in to see you on Monday morning, I didn't think you'd welcome a visit at the weekend.'

'Monday will do fine,' Kelsey said as he came up. 'There's just one point I'd like to clear up now. We've been chatting to your wife up at the church and she tells us she didn't actually collect you at four-thirty that last Friday at the school.'

Lloyd frowned. 'But she did, surely—'

'She says she had Barry Finch with her in the car, she was late, so she looked in at the school to tell you—'

Lloyd raised a hand. 'Of course, I remember now, she's quite right.' He looked apologetic. 'I'm terribly sorry, I'm afraid it completely slipped my mind.'

'Not to worry,' Kelsey said. 'But perhaps you'd cast your mind back now, try to be exact in what you recall.'

'I'll certainly do my best.'

'When your wife left the school at four-thirty to take Barry home, did you remain in your office?'

'No,' Lloyd said at once. 'I took the opportunity to clear out a cupboard in my classroom.'

'What precisely did you do?'

Lloyd stared up into the boughs of an apple-tree. On the topmost branch a blackbird sang, liquid and trilling.

'I closed the window in the office, then my wife and I left the office and I closed the door. We walked along to my classroom, talking, then my wife went off. I stayed in the classroom doing the cupboard, I'd just about finished when she came back.'

'And that would be at what time?'

'She came back at about a quarter past, twenty past five.'

'And you remained in your classroom the whole time she was away? You didn't go back into the office at all?'

'No, I stayed in the classroom. When she came back I closed the classroom and she helped me carry the exhibition things from the hall out to the car. Then I locked up and we drove home.'

'When you closed the office window at four-thirty, did you see anyone outside? In the field?'

'Just the two Mayfield men working on the fencing. No one else.'

'And in the three-quarters of an hour you were in your classroom, did you hear or see anything at all unusual?'

Lloyd shook his head. 'No, nothing.'

'Right,' Kelsey said. 'You've been very helpful.'

They walked back up the garden. As they drew near the house they heard the sound of a car turning in through the gates—Mrs Lloyd, returned for more fern and foliage.

'You found Henry all right?' she called out as they came up. She jumped out, picked up some empty containers from the passenger seat and set them down on the gravel. She went round to the back of the vehicle and began to take out jugs and vases.

'Yes, thank you,' Kelsey called back. He repressed a groan. 'We're trapped,' he said to Lambert in a bleak undertone—the station wagon was blocking their car.

Mrs Lloyd thrust a couple of vases at the Chief. 'If you wouldn't mind taking these inside the house for me,' she said briskly. 'I'll be as quick as I can, out of your way.'

She glanced at Lambert, a useful pair of hands doing nothing. 'Would you be kind enough to bring along some of these? I'll be finished all the sooner.'

She led the way into the house through a side door, along a passage to a garden room, thick-walled, with a stone-flagged floor, full of the scents of flowers and foliage. Wellingtons were ranged against the walls, the shelves were crowded with balls of twine, labels, gardening gloves. Jugs of montbretia and gypsophila stood on the floor by an old glazed earthenware sink.

'Always lovely and cool in here,' Mrs Lloyd said. 'Even in the heat.' She glanced at their burdens. 'You can put those down over there. The baskets go on the hooks.'

They dutifully followed her instructions. One of the baskets was rather striking in appearance, shallow and circular, with two oval handles, woven in a gaily-coloured intricate pattern.

She saw the Chief admire it. 'It's an unusual design,' she said. 'An interesting example of that particular weave. My cousin gave it to me, her son brought it back from the Argentine. I lent it to the craft exhibition at the school—I lent them a number of items, that pottery jar over there was one of them.' She indicated a jar of a beautiful soft dull turquoise standing on a shelf, the handles shaped like lizards. 'That came from Peru, it belonged to my grandfather.'

She thrust a jug of fern at Sergeant Lambert. 'Would you be kind enough to take that out to the car for me?'

When she had finally driven off, Kelsey went back to the garden room and took the basket down from its hook.

'This looks to me,' he said, 'as if it could be the basket Janet Marshall borrowed from Lloyd that last day at school.'

Lambert took the basket and looked at it. 'If it is,' he said, 'then she must have taken it back to the school, the Lloyds would have picked it up with the rest of the exhibition stuff.'

'Looks like it.' Kelsey twisted his mouth into elaborate shapes. 'If she went across the field and slipped in at the back door of the school Lloyd wouldn't see her if he was busy in his classroom. She sees the exhibition stuff still in the hall, she drops the basket in amongst it and goes off again.' He frowned. 'That does suggest that she was alone in the cottage at that point, that the murderer wasn't inside, waiting for her, when she got home from school.'

'He could have been hanging about outside somewhere,' Lambert suggested. 'In the shed, perhaps. He sees her come out of the back door carrying the basket, she wouldn't bother to lock the door, not if she was only going to be away a minute or two. He dodges inside and waits for her to get back.' He paused. 'How does that affect Schofield? Does it seem to let him out?'

Kelsey gave a noncommittal grunt. 'One thing's for sure, it doesn't let Ken Bryant out.' He ran a finger along his top lip. 'Neil Fleming had already gone up to the farmhouse. Janet comes out of the back door with the basket, she starts to cross the field towards the school. Bryant is still working on the fencing, he sees her approach, he speaks to her. He says: You'll be off on your holidays, no doubt? She says Yes. He says: Could I have a word with you about Jill's maths before you go? I'd like to fix something up. She says: Yes, certainly, I won't be a moment. I've just got to drop this in at the school and then we can settle things. She comes back almost at once and walks back to Rose Cottage with Bryant. There's no one around to see.'

'This could be the basket,' Lambert said. 'I can't recollect any basket in Rose Cottage.'

'We can soon check.' Kelsey flexed his shoulders. 'We'll pop down the garden again and ask Lloyd.'

The headmaster was slashing at a patch of weeds under the apple-trees as they walked down the path a second time. Overhead the blackbird sang sweetly and ardently.

Lloyd was stooping with his back to them. Kelsey could see the bald crown of his head, brown and shiny in the late afternoon sunshine. His shirtsleeves were rolled up, his arms were deeply tanned. He made a sweeping turn with his billhook and caught sight of them.

'This basket—' Kelsey said in explanation as they came up; he held the basket out.

Then he saw the expression on Lloyd's face, his look as he saw the basket. He felt the hairs stiffen along the back of his neck. Hold hard, a voice said inside his head, hold hard. He came to an abrupt halt.

Lloyd remained motionless with the billhook held out, ready for the next swing. Sergeant Lambert eyed the blade, glittering, razor-sharp.

'You went back to your office when your wife drove off,' Kelsey said, working it out. 'You looked out of the window and saw that the two workmen were no longer there.' Fleming up at the house, Bryant gone off to the turkey sheds. 'You concluded they'd finished for the day. You went down to Rose Cottage and Janet opened the door. You said: I've come to pick up the basket. She let you in.'

Lloyd stood looking at them, silent, rigid. On his lean brown forearms the veins stood out like cords.

'Tell me about it,' the Chief said gently.

Lloyd suddenly threw down the billhook with a gesture of finality. He stood with his arms hanging loosely at his sides, looking down at the ravaged grass.

'She was always there,' he said at last. 'Every day. But I never saw her alone.' He drew a long, shuddering breath. 'I meant her no harm. She got hysterical, she started to scream, she called me terrible things, she wouldn't stop.' He dropped his head into his hands. 'I don't remember much—I didn't know what to do. I had to get back to the school. I put her on the stairs. I put the curtain over her and closed the door. I picked up the basket and went back across the field.'

He began to cry. 'I just wanted her to be kind to me. To have had something out of it all. Not to have done it all for nothing.'

Kelsey put a hand on his arm and Lloyd offered no resistance. They turned to walk up to the car. Under their feet the slashed weeds, thick and moist, gave off a sharp fresh scent. A breeze sprang up in the branches of a philadelphus and a shower of petals fluttered down, falling about them like snow. In the apple-tree the blackbird went on singing.